THE LAME OLD MAN

THE LAME OLD MAN

Marwan Al Bakheet

Translated from Arabic by
Haya Nafez Thabet

NOMAD
PUBLISHING

THE LAME OLD MAN

Marwan Al Bakheet

Published by Nomad Publishing in 2023
Email: info@nomad-publishing.com
www.nomad-publishing.com
Cover design: Lucie Wimetz

ISBN 9781914325496

 The Publishers would like
to thank the Harf Literary Agency

Printed in India by Imprint Press

Contents

Preface

Among all the cluttered shelves in that modest room, one shelf is exceptionally tidy and organised. It is embraced in holiness, revered and appreciated.

Even if there is space for it, nothing deserves to be added to that shelf unless it has justified its place.

I sit in front of it and engross myself in its realms, gulp from its springs, and learn from its knowledge.

I frequently seclude myself there, laughing until my eyes are filled with tears, encountering a funny story in a novel, cheering a deep statement in an article, or humming with delight at an enchanting verse of poetry. No one is allowed to share my solitude or my writings, in that modest room beside a lonely corner shelf.

Dedication

To Doctor Ghazi Abdul Rahman Al Gosaibi,
God bless his soul.
To the man who can no longer see the people he
helped to grow, and who I can no longer dream of
meeting. To you, Abu Yara.
Also to that shelf - to the holiness it holds, and to the
different realms it embraces.

A Note

All the incidents and depictions included in this book are based on pure imagination and have nothing to do with reality in any way. Any resemblance to reality is a mere coincidence.

The Author

"And the moon we estimated it for stages until

it returned like the old [lame] date stalk."

Surah Yasin, 36 verse.

PART ONE
THE PALM POLLEN

Oh, generous palm tree!

Mercy and peace be upon you.

Chapter 1

"Hello, I'm Jalal."

He stood in front of a spice shop at Al-Qaisareya's big traditional market. It was a hot and suffocating day; he was wiping off the sweat that was dripping from his face. It was 4pm, and the heat of the sun should have started to fade by this time of day but that fact didn't seem to apply to this part of the world.

"I phoned you earlier to confirm the booking of some items," he said, after taking off his red shemagh (headdress) and using his already wet handkerchief to wipe his forehead and the wide bridge of his nose. The front of his bald head was exposed, bathed in sweat.

The shop assistant disappeared inside the small shop. Jalal took a deep breath until his chest was filled with the scent of herbs that permeated every corner of the place. Cinnamon, saffron, fennel, harmal, ginger, and quantities of popular spices and perfumes, whose fragrance spread into the crowded lands of the old market.

Nothing could spoil his mood while he inhaled his favourite scents, except the reflection he could see in a small dirty mirror that was fixed on the corner of the shop. He felt a little upset when he saw his face. His thick eyebrows seemed to be knitted together and his long beard looked very messy, with grey hair sneaking in from behind and peeking out in between the black. He must go to the barbershop and have his hair cut, he thought to himself.

This was a very special day for him and his family - it was his wedding anniversary. He had to be well dressed and look the part. Everything had to be perfect.

He waited at the doorway with irritation, scratching his chin until the assistant finally appeared from inside the shop holding several small brown paper bags. Jalal examined them, then sniffed the contents to test their quality, and when satisfied, left the shop and walked along the narrow lanes of the old market.

This place, with its high mud walls and decades of history, had always been special and dear to his heart. A majestic ottoman design, scents and smells poured out of the stores and shops that lined its labyrinthine passageways. Every single inch of it was steeped in originality.

The market had numerous gates of Islamic design that welcomed visitors who came from outside the city of Al-Ahsa. Elderly people dressed in traditional clothes gave it a historical presence, an ongoing connection with the past.

"Jalal?"

A voice suddenly came from behind him, and he was

shocked when he recognised the owner of the sound. It was a voice he had never forgotten, rooted and engraved in the depth of his heart.

"Ghassan Al-Kaheil?"

He rushed to him, not able to believe the sight his eyes were capturing. Ghassan had been standing beside Al-Sayed's café when he came out and hugged him tight.

Their last embrace had been 30 years ago and he had missed his friend so badly. Seeing him revived floods of memories and overwhelmed with emotions, his eyes sparkled with tears. At that moment, he could not see nor hear anything except Ghassan. He needed to know all that had happened to him over the past three decades. So much must have taken place and he had missed it all.

Ghassan certainly looked very different from the last time they had met each other. Time had printed eternally visible marks on his face and he looked older than his real age. There was now an obvious age difference between the two friends with Jalal looking notably younger than Ghassan.

His friend was still wearing the same rounded glasses with thin golden frames, however, and he still had the same delicate eyebrows that were artfully drawn over his eyes. Those eyes were the same - always a little watery, giving people the feeling that he was going to burst into tears at any moment.

Ghassan's previously short beard looked a bit longer than it used to be. He also had grey hairs scattered amongst it, but they seemed to match in well with his white ghutra (headdress). He had gained some weight and his slacked cheeks made him look like a solemn sheikh.

"I can't believe my eyes. I have finally found you! I thought I had lost you forever," said Jalal.

The noise of the crowded lanes was hampering their reminisces, forcing them to go to a café. They sat on wooden chairs opposite each other around a small old worn-out table that seemed to be imbued with misery and bitterness at life.

Ghassan took a sip from a glass of water before saying,

"What a coincidence! Better than a thousand appointments. If I had arrived late, I would have missed the chance of seeing you. I couldn't believe that the man standing among all those people was Jalal Al-Rameh."

"We really missed you. We thought that something bad had happened to you when you left the city," said Jalal.

Ghassan lowered his head.

"This wasn't easy for me. You know what really forced me to leave," he said bitterly.

Jalal could sense the depth of sadness in his friend, so he quickly changed the subject.

"After you left, I was keen to know all your news from your father," he said. "I used to visit him every now and then to ask him if there were any calls or messages from you. But no news came. What happened? And where have you been all that time? Was it easy for you to leave all our childhood memories behind?"

Ghassan shook his head, trying to defend himself and deny the accusations. "I do not disparage our memories, nor our friendship, Jalal. But as you have just said, there were tough years. I had to go through many struggles, and I give thanks to Allah for everything that I have now."

Jalal was silent for a moment and started contemplating his friend's face that had changed so much over time. He thought about their friendship and how all the means of communication between them had been stopped. He whispered the question had always puzzled him.

"Why didn't you come to visit me?"

Ghassan focused his eyes on the glass of water in front of him, inhaled a deep breath and said,

"I left 30 years ago and this is only my second visit to Al-Ahsa after many long years of absence. One of those times was to attend the ceremonies of my father's funeral, God bless his soul, and I stayed for only one day. I had to go back to where I was."

There was a heavy moment of silence, finally dispersed by the shouts of a vendor promoting his goods in the street outside. Jalal felt the grief lingering in his friend's eyes, which triggered his own sad memories as well. He wanted the awkwardness to end, and spoke in a more encouraging tone.

"What matters is that you are here now. There are so many things we need to talk about, but not here and not now. This is not the right place and not the right timing, either. We must agree on an appointment to meet as soon as possible."

"I don't have much time," Ghassan replied. "I'm only on a brief duty here in the Kingdom and I thought I would seize this opportunity to perform Umrah before paying a short visit to Al-Ahsa. And I wanted to visit this market, as I am staying at the Intercontinental Hotel nearby. My flight is scheduled before eight o'clock tomorrow morning, Saturday, I mean. Then, I'm leaving again."

Jalal was astounded and could not hide the feeling of rejection creeping over his face. "Leave! So soon? Haven't you had enough of all that bitter alienation? Don't you think it's time to cast off the dust from travelling and settle in your homeland once again?"

Ghassan sighed, clearly not enjoying the question.

"I don't have anything or anyone to remain here for," he said, heavily, trying to justify his point. "All my life has shifted, and there I should be, not here."

"Alright," Jalal replied. "Just don't expect me to let you go so easily. We should meet at my house this evening."

Ghassan looked uncomfortable.

"I'm not sure if it is a good idea, my friend," he said, reluctantly.

Jalal took off his glasses, adjusted himself in his seat, and spoke in a very serious tone.

"How could I meet my best friend after 30 years of absence and just let him go? Do you think a brief meeting of only a few minutes is enough? We don't have many more years to live, my friend, and there is no guarantee that we would ever bump into each other like this again. No, this is impossible!

I will tell you how things will go. I will leave now, and you will come to my house tonight. I want all of my family to meet my best friend, whom I have known since my early childhood. I also want you to meet them."

The discussion concluded with Ghassan giving up his protests and accepting the invitation of the man who long ago had been his best friend.

How he longed to go back in time to those early years. Memories of that time had given him comfort during his time away, soothing him whenever he felt distressed. When thoughts of those days came into his mind without warning, he could not help but cry out in longing and pain for times gone by.

They both parted after agreeing to meet again that night.

Chapter 2

When the clock that hung on the wall in Jalal's house pointed at eight-thirty that night, everything was as it should be.

A sound was coming from one of the rooms. It wasn't an unusual one - it was often heard in the house, and its owner was a member of the family.

Jalal was standing in front of a large mirror in his bedroom. He was looking at his reflection and humming along with a melody emitting from a speaker placed in the corner. The singsong voice of his favourite singer was filling the room.

"I'm coming back to see you...

I was driven by my longing....

I'm wondering how you are…

And how night influenced you…"

"You never have enough of Talal's songs!," laughed his wife as she entered the room. She was drying her wet hair and she knew that singing was a clear indication that her husband was in a good mood. In fact, he was over the moon.

He ignored her teasing and walked towards her, wrapping his arms around her petite body. He kissed her on the forehead and whispered in her ear while looking at her lovingly.

"Many happy returns, baby, and happy anniversary. On this day, 33 years ago, it was officially announced that every day for the rest of my life would be one of festivity with you."

Lameya's face beamed with a shy smile, as usual. The years had made their marks on her face, but she still had beautiful features, her eyes holding a child's innocence, a small mole sitting like a crown on her upper lip that was often the target of her husband's flirting and teasing in a way that caused her much embarrassment. She had gained some additional kilos over time because of repeated pregnancies and while her hair had kept its dark blackness, it had lost thickness and in some areas it had become very thin, making every attempt to style her hair on special occasions a time to lament her passing years.

He pulled her towards him.

"Today, in this house, we are celebrating our anniversary together with our small family that we have worked hard to establish and preserve through the years," he said.

"I'm overwhelmed with blessings, and I cannot but be thankful. I feel I'm the most blessed man in the world and the most fortunate as well. And you, Lameya, are the most exceptional blessing I have."

She turned scarlet as her fair cheeks blushed. She was used to her husband stating how he felt about her in the most intimate ways, but she would always stay silent, unable to find the appropriate words to respond. But he didn't mind. He had once told her that she did not need to expose herself and disclose how she felt because she was able to show her love through her actions and her attentions. The shyness residing in her eyes was more eloquent and beyond any words she might articulate with words, he had said.

He looked into eyes.

"Do you want me to bring the oxygen cylinder to the ground floor?" he asked, tenderly.

She shook her head, saying she did not need it.

"What about your medicine? Have you already taken your pills?"

"The same questions every single day!" she scolded. "Yes, I have taken them all and feel much better and I don't feel I need the oxygen cylinder. Are you happy now?"

Jalal smiled while still drowning in her eyes. A moment of dreamy silence passed between them before Lameya interrupted him with a whisper.

"We can stay here like this all night and forget about the celebration and about those who are waiting for us downstairs. But they will end up breaking into the room at any moment and will get in by force!"

She hardly finished her words when they heard someone knocking at the door. It was an informal knock and whoever was behind the door was clearly not waiting for permission to enter, as it opened immediately before either Lemaya or Jalal could respond.

"You are still here! What are you doing?"

Their son dashed into the room, but his mother pushed him back gently with her hand.

"We're fed up with waiting downstairs!" the boy said impatiently.

"What have I told you, Khatir?" she reproached.

Lameya turned to her husband, who went to finish dressing, then turned to her son.

"How many times do I have to remind you, Khatir? You are no longer a child. You are more than 12 years old now and you should not dash into rooms before you are permitted to do so."

Khatir ignored his mother's ticking off and began to grumble about being bored and having to kill time by himself. His mother promised she would follow him downstairs in a few minutes and then closed the door in his face.

"I swear I will sleep in your bed tonight if you don't both get down to the ground floor immediately, do you understand?" Khatir shouted behind the closed door of his parent's bedroom. He could hear his father's humming inside the room.

"And the dreams made us forget the days of bitter quarrels,
    And I'm coming to see you!"

Chapter 3

The sitting room was decorated with colourful fabric and flowers. The smell from the incense wafted around the whole place. A rectangular table was arranged in the middle of the room, on which coffee, tea, fresh juice and fancy chocolate were neatly placed. In the middle of the table was a round cake with a picture of Jalal's smiling face printed on it, decorated with lines of liquid chocolate.

When Jalal and Lameya started to walk down the stairs, the sound of music rose from the sitting room, brightly coloured ribbons were fired into the air, and joy shone on everybody's faces. The gathered family jumped to their feet to congratulate their parents on their anniversary. The first was their eldest, their daughter Sara, who had made them a grandfather and grandmother. She was holding their grandsons, one with her hand and the other still inside her body. Sara kissed her parents on the head and then carried her son, five year old Basim, to have a kiss from his kind grandparents.

In his usual polite style, Sara's husband, Ali, stepped forward to congratulate them, remarking with admiration on their impressive harmony over so many years and their ability to overcome all the difficulties and challenges they had encountered.

Lameya sat next to her husband. She was dressed in a shining scarlet jalabiya and had an ornamental ivory shawl on her shoulders that she often wore when her daughter's husband visited them.

The whole family celebrated the occasion with loud music playing. All hands held the knife that cut the cake, and then they all gathered in the sitting room talking and laughing. Love dominated the place.

"When is my new grandson arriving, Sara? I can't wait to see him," Jalal said while shoving another piece of cake onto his plate.

"It seems that you like the idea of being a grandfather a lot, Jalal! Don't count me in with you. You are 55 years old now. I'm still enjoying my youth, while you have left youth behind you," laughed Lameya, laying down a gauntlet to Jalal to respond. He put his plate on the table in front of him before defending himself.

"It seems that you grow younger every year, my dear, instead of growing older," he joked back. "We are celebrating our 33rd anniversary today! You have to face the truth now; you have already become a grandmother and you have grandsons."

"That doesn't prove anything. Did you forget that I married you at a very young age? You kidnapped me when I was only seventeen and..."

Her husband bent his body towards her and kept teasing.

"Roses are not kidnapped, my dear. They are picked!"

Their son-in-law ended the moment of flirting that had made Lameya blush and look aside, pretending not to care.

"I feel proud to see you living in such harmony after being together all these years," Ali said, full of admiration. "No-one would think you are approaching your sixties, uncle. Of course, this does not apply in any way to my aunt. It seems that she is still in her twenties, according to her calendar."

Jalal burst into laughter, his body vibrating, as he intentionally exaggerated his reaction to his son-in-law.

"I have always loved this guy, and my love for him grows day after day," he said, full of jesting sarcasm. "You speak the truth, my son, you always do that."

Jalal laughed again, irritating Lameya who usually tried to ignore this sort of directly provocative behaviour. She turned to Sara.

"So, you have married a man who looks like your father, alright. I have always felt that you have not been that fortunate in this life, my daughter."

Everyone burst into laughter. The family members took delight in this teasing, which had become one of the regular traditions of every family gathering, in addition to the naughty behaviour of Basim and Khatir.

Khatir was sitting in his favourite place, next to his mother, wrapping his arms around her and resting his left cheek on her shoulder. She was chatting to his sister when he put his hand on his mother's right breast. Lameya was shocked, and her face grew red. She pushed his hand away angrily, and reproached him in the presence of all the disapproving eyes.

His face stiffened with embarrassment and a vein between his eyebrows in the middle of his forehead began to throb. He was overwhelmed with fury, jumping to his feet and leaving the room. Seconds later, they heard the door of the kitchen slam as he headed for his secret hideout outside the house.

Khatir was attached to his mother more than any other member of the family and Lameya always paid him much attention. Sara had been born not long after their marriage, bringing joy and happiness to their life. But things did not go the same easy way afterwards. They waited a long time to have their second baby. It was a difficult journey filled with many tests, examinations and unsuccessful pregnancies. Eventually their dreams came true and Khatir arrived.

The delivery was difficult, however, and both the baby and Lameya's life were in jeopardy during the process. Having survived all of this, he had secured a special place in his mother's heart and consequently, enjoyed the biggest portion of her love, care, and attention.

Awkwardness had fallen over the room after Khatir's departure and Lemaya, Sara and Basim went upstairs. The silence left behind was relieved by the sound of the doorbell. Ali volunteered to check on who was there, and he came back announcing the coming of a guest, Ghassan Al-Kaheil.

Chapter 4

The two old friends hugged each other again, as tightly as they had done earlier that day outside the cafe. Ghassan was dressed elegantly but simply, his beard was cut and styled especially for this visit, a white headdress on which a very dark black agal was placed, an elegant glowing white jalabiya reaching his ankles, and plain black shoes, shined to a high polish. Ali served coffee for the guest and for his father-in-law, then served dates covered with molasses.

"I beg your pardon," Jalal apologised to Ghassan as he placed a cup of coffee on the small table in front of him. He pointed at Ali.

"I have forgotten to introduce my son-in-law, he is like

my true son," Jalal said. . He is Mr Ali, a lecturer at the university and a researcher in the field of psychology. We will be delighted when he completes his final research - we are all very proud of him."

Ali sat on a chair opposite them in his usual calm manner. He had a quiet, charming smile on his face that reflected his inner confidence and peaceful character. Ghassan interrupted Jalal and addressed Ali in admiration.

"God bless you. So you are one of those who enjoy analysing personalities , revealing the hidden sides of human beings through the way they look and behave. And always call for optimism and living life to its fullest," said Ghassan.

The smile on Ali's face widened.

"Yes, to some extent I'm as you described," he responded. "But I don't agree with the part about excessive hope and optimism."

Ali took a sip from the cup of coffee in front of him.

"From a personal perspective," he added, "I have considerable reservations about those who look at life through rose-tinted spectacles, thinking that everything they want will be achieved and all they need is just to insist on having it. This is wrong and ridiculous."

"I don't think many of the people in your field think in this way, and I do agree with your perspective," Jalal said, urging his son-in-law to say more.

Ali went on.

"Some people reach a stage of self-deceit and behave in a misleading way, and this is the point of disagreement. If we urge people to consider the positive part of everything, then we should, in the same way, encourage them to look at the gloomier sides too, so that they will be able to make sound judgments and make the right decisions."

The young man, seeing that he could hold the attention of his father-in-law and the guest as well, felt encouraged to digress.

"For example, if a certain young man dreamed of being a famous writer, and took a particularly successful famous writer as a role model for himself, he would actually have no idea that behind every successful famous writer, there are a hundred writers whose books are never sold. And behind them, there are another hundred writers who are still looking for a publishing company, and behind those, there are another hundred with drafts covered with dust in drawers. And behind them, there are hundreds more who are just dreaming of being famous writers one day and have not yet written a word!

"You can measure this at different levels and with different ambitions. So if you want something, you must look at the graveyard that holds the dreams of those who tried but failed, as well as looking at those who end up celebrated with their names in lights, having succeeded with flying colours."

Ghassan nodded his head, approving of what he had just heard.

"We have never been taught that we should think this way," he said. "People with specialist knowledge should raise awareness in this regard."

Jalal objected, although he knew that his son-in-law was right.

"That's right," he said, after taking a sip of coffee. "But disseminating such frustrating ideas among people is not appropriate, or palatable for many anyway."

Ali answered quickly.

"We have to present the truth, which is not what we always want to hear. Yes, I agree that it is harsh sometimes and not always palatable, but it is real."

Jalal was impressed. Filled with admiration for his son-in-law, he smiled and turned his head to Ghassan, saying proudly,

"Now you see why I selected him as a husband to my daughter!"

A wry smile crept over Ghassan's face.

"I don't doubt that," he murmured. "And I have to admit that I'm impressed by him as well. But were you sure that he didn't take something that belonged to someone else?"

A moment of confused silence filled the room. Jalal and his son-in-law exchanged puzzled looks.

"How can anyone take something that belongs to another?" Jalal said. "Every one of us gets his full share of this life, my friend."

"Not necessarily, some people are so greedy, they are never satisfied with what they have and they won't hesitate to steal what is in the hands of others!"

Jalal paused.

"What are you talking about, Ghassan? I don't think I understand what you mean."

The guest scratched his beard.

"I don't mean anything at all," Ghassan said. "This is just passing talk about those people whose selfishness knows no bounds, so they will do anything to get what they want, by any means. Even if they have to steal their friend's wives! I like your son-in-law a lot, but I just wanted to make sure he did not marry another man's girl."

Ali grew angry and interrupted Ghassan.

"Have some respect for yourself and for the people to whom you are talking, man! Think of your words before saying them. What are you talking about?"

"I apologise, Mr Ali. I'm as shocked as you when I encounter people who never stop acting strangely in every stage of their lives. "

Jalal's face turned gloomy, as he understood the hidden message behind Ghassan's words. He sighed deeply.

"You can never forget this!," he said to his friend. "I thought that all the many years that had elapsed would have washed your heart and soul, but it seems that you haven't changed. Your heart flows with venom, hatred and malice. That happened long ago, and I haven't invited you here today to talk about something that will cloud our meeting and our friendship!"

Ghassan let out a sarcastic laugh and interrupted him with a loud voice.

"Cloud our friendship! You are talking about friendship? You could not wait to bring a knife and stab me from behind! What friendship are you talking about, selfish man?

All those years of alienation did not manage to make me forget your treachery."

Jalal hands began to shake anxiously and he spoke in a louder, nervous voice. ,

"You can't cast the malice from your eyes to be able to see the truth in front of you, no matter how much you make yourself a pious ascetic by dressing and looking this way!

"I was mistaken to have invited you to my house, especially someone who has a dangerous criminal and security record like you have. Do you want me to remind you of the reasons behind your continuous travelling and migration from your homeland?"

Ghassan threw down the cup of coffee, spilling its contents on the table in front of him. He jumped to his feet in fury and screamed,

"Being invited into this house does not grant me any honour at all. You don't know the meaning of friendship, and if I knew that I would have the misfortune to meet with you again, I would prefer to die there and then, far away from your damned face.

"Yes," Jalal shouted back, "death would be more merciful than seeing your face again."

Shouts clamoured from the room as the former friends turned opponents exchanged insults and accusations. The silence that had reigned over them for more than three decades burst open, the bonds of love and friendship were torn and the friendship that embraced the meeting moments ago turned into rage. The place was more like a wrestling ring, curses flying, while Ali desperately failed in his attempts to calm them down.

"I swear to God that you will never taste a blessing from now on, I will make you taste pain and deprivation in the same way that you did to me. You don't deserve her, Jalal. You don't deserve her," Ghassan shouted.

He had barely finished his threat when Jalal pushed him hard towards the door, his face red in fury. Ghassan lost his balance for a moment and his gold-rimmed glasses fell to the ground. As soon as he picked them up, he headed for the door, boiling with anger. When he reached the corridor leading to the outer door, he saw Lameya standing in the middle of the stairs, shock and fear on her face at the noise of all the commotion taking place below..

Their eyes met for a few fleeting seconds, but in those seconds, a whole lifetime passed by. All the memories, all the moments, and all the dreams that once were and had now passed over. She quickly threw her veil on her face. At the same time, Ghassan woke up from his daydream that had lasted for just a few heartbeats and left the house, miserable and humiliated.

The scene that had just been laid out in front of Lameya was almost incomprehensible to her. Just a moment ago, her husband was fighting with her ex-fiancée. In her house!

Chapter 5

A state of awkwardness and tension lay over everyone in a way they had never experienced before. There was silence, and no one dared to utter a word and crack the quiet that had descended.

Jalal sat down and took off his white headdress, casting it on the sofa next to him. Sara rushed to bring him a glass of water, hoping to calm her furious father down. Lameya sat in silence in the corner, wrapping her ivory shawl around her tightly, her feet shaking with anxiety. Khatir was by her side. She was astounded by who she had just seen in the hallway. She never thought she would ever see Ghassan again, and after all these years, his existence in her imagination had completely vanished.

"Calm down, uncle, you have done nothing to warrant worrying about," Ali said, himself a little anxiously, as he was concerned for Jalal's health. Jalal's hands trembled, as he drank water from the glass.

Then, looking at the space in front of him, he said, "I curse the moment I met him. He has turned our special night into hell, damn him."

"You should not curse people in this way!"

Lameya spoke calmly from the corner of the sitting room, her steady tone contrasting sharply with his trembling voice. He turned to her, as if she, too, was about to spoil the whole evening.

"Oh! You are defending him, are you? It seems that you long for your old love!"

A gloom fell on the faces of all the members of his family, for it was such a serious and direct accusation. Lameya's eyebrows shivered for a second.

"I don't care about him or about any other one," she said. "Cursing is unacceptable, that is all. Our children are sitting with us, and it is not a good idea for them to hear such things, especially from their father."

Ali spoke up, trying to dissipate the tension in the room.

"We should all try to calm down now. We are all extremely anxious and upset - and no one should say anything that he might later regret."

Everyone kept silent, but Jalal was boiling with rage on the inside and he would not relax until he exploded. So he ignored the words of his son-in-law and spoke again to his wife.

"What made you come down to the ground floor? Who permitted you to do so?"

Lameya looked at the ground, ignoring his question. Then Sara said, in a hesitant, defensive tone, "We were worried when we heard raised voices and shouts. We thought something serious might be going on, so we went to explore the situation. That's it!"

"Oh, you were worried, were you?" Jalal responded, his voice full of sarcasm, determined to be provoked.

"Were you really worried? Or had you heard his voice from upstairs and that triggered your longing, so you wanted to see him and quench your thirst for him?"

"What are you talking about, Jalal? How dare you say this or even think of such a thing?"

Lameya shouted while tears filled her eyes, smarting at the unfair accusations being thrown at her. Jalal would not back down.

"Do you want to convince me that your presence at that exact time and letting him see you face-to-face was just an innocent coincidence? Your behaviour is shameful for someone of your age."

"You have gone too far, Jalal," she cried. "This is too much. Have you forgotten that I have been your wife for more than 30 years and I'm the mother of your children? Have you forgotten that?"

She stood up, feeling a mixture of distress and humiliation and headed for the stairs. Jalal jumped to his feet and stepped towards her.

"No, I haven't forgotten that. But I also have not forgotten the emotional history that joins you and him! Do you wish things had worked out differently and that you belonged only to him?"

Her features were frozen in shock. She looked him in the eye and walked to him slowly, while everyone in the room looked on.

"If that brings comfort to your heart and heals your anger, then yes. I wish that had really happened!"

A flash of pain penetrated her cheek as Jalal slapped her, his anger spilling over from boiling point. A tear fell on her face, exposing a vulnerability that she was trying hard to hide behind stern facial expressions.

Silence hung in the air, with the eyes of all the onlookers about to pop out of their sockets. Sara, Ali, Basim, and Khatir had never witnessed such violence in their lives.

Lameya pushed the hair away from her face exposing her

red cheek, looking at her husband in a way that was more painful than the slap he had delivered.

"It seems that my father was not mistaken when he warned me not to give you all my money. It's not over, though, and this mistake can be fixed!"

She turned her back without another word and climbed the stairs in defiant steps.

So the worst night the family had ever experienced ended. Khatir followed his mother, tears filling his eyes. He was deeply affected by what he had just witnessed, and his father's unforgivable deed. The veins in his face were throbbing.

"You are the worst father ever!," he shouted at his father amid his tears.

Then he dashed up the stairs. Meanwhile, Ali gestured to his wife that they should go home. He felt embarrassed and was fully aware that being a witness to that situation had aggravated its intensity and awkwardness. He dearly wished he were not there.

Sara picked up her things and quickly gathered her child's toys, leaving her father alone in the sitting room.

The house that had been so noisy with laughter and love only a few hours ago was now silent. The decorative lights were still glittering on the ceiling in colours that were at first full of joy but now seemed to cast a shadow of gloom on Jalal as he sat by himself. The cake with his face printed on it was still on the table, but his smile seemed foolish and misplaced at that moment.

His head was filled with ideas, wonderings and questions. He threw his body on the sofa and raked over the events that had unfolded that night - the coincidence of meeting Ghassan, his insistence on inviting him to his house, the quarrel with him, the malice that was directed to him, slapping Lameya on the face. How did all that happen?"

He took off his jalabiya and lay down staring at the ceiling for a while, before falling asleep from exhaustion. The whole house was so quiet after the storm, silence was the master of the night and its prince.

The early hours of the next day, they all woke up to one fact. A devastating fact.

Lameya was not in the house. She was gone!

PART TWO
THE ROOTS

"Like a good tree, whose root is firmly fixed

and its branches [high] in the sky."

Surat Ibrahim (Abraham), Verse (14)

Chapter 6

A soft cool breeze shivered across the trunks of the graceful palm trees, producing a soothing rustling sound. The thick tangled leaves swayed like clasping hands and almost blocked the sunlight. The scent of wet soil spread and blended with the sound of the babbling freshwater spring.

The day was done, and the sky was getting ready for the eternal journey of sunset. The clock announced my regular weekly appointment at four o'clock in the afternoon.

There, in the corner of the mud wall, was a worn-out rectangular iron plate. The blue paint that had covered it had faded, making it hard to read the name engraved on it. But when the sunlight reflected on the water and shined on that plate, the name (Ein Om Zanbour) could be read. It was the most visited place in the village, especially at this scorching time of the year.

On the other side, on the front of the wall, a patriotic statement was written in bad handwriting. Long Live King Khalid. I started to take off my clothes in haste, I was overwhelmed with longing for the cool waters that awaited me.

Selecting this time of day was not haphazard or random. It was carefully chosen as it preceded the crowds who came to cool down and relax in the springs. I wanted to enjoy a swim in the clean water before all the other people polluted it.

"Are you kidding me, Jalal? I don't believe that you still have that costume!"

The sound came from behind me while I unzipped my green tracksuit, exposing my scrawny body with protruding ribs. I cast the tracksuit aside, then turned around and smiled.

"Not only that, Ghassan," I said, "I still have all the gifts we used to have from King Khalid at school. The pencils, the notebooks, the shoes as well as the sports clothes they used to give to everyone. Not all of us can always buy new sports clothes as you and your family do, my dear. My father does not earn as much as your father does."

Ghassan started to hang his clothes on the palm tree trunk, before putting on some white trunks.

"I remember the exhilarating joy when he sent the school a table tennis table as a gift for high achievers," he said. "I was one of them and the room where they placed the table was our small heaven."

"It was a shame that you were so elated and comfortable that you forgot your friend, who was stuck outside the room and not allowed to get in. Damn you, maths! Without it causing me problems, I would have joined the club. And if that had happened, I would have made you lose badly!"

Ghassan ignored my last remark because it was time for

fun, specifically jumping into the refreshing water. It was the weekly moment we agreed on, and could not miss whatever happened. That moment was our personal reimbursement after the exhaustion of the week. We stood at the edge of the spring filled with joy, our bare feet touching the wet ground. We closed our eyes and inhaled a deep breath, filling our lungs with the scent of palm trees.

"Look, who we found here!"

The sound came from behind the trees, spoiling our moment of pleasure and heralding the arrival of trouble. The timing could not have been worse.

"What are you doing here at this time?" The sound came from a rusty throat, backed up by a team of bullies.

Awad was a beefy guy with a big body and dark skin. He came from the neighbouring village, Materfi.. Both Al-Shaqiq and Materfi had once been one village and one family in the past, but there had been a conflict over palm trees, land and crops, especially when some nomads had come looking for water and food. The conflict became serious, and despite years of living harmoniously together, with long standing intermarriages and family connections, the people who belonged to the Materfi family parted from Al Shaqiq. Afterwards, each village prevented people from the other village from crossing their lands and those who dared to challenge this were severely punished.

One day, the two villages woke up to news that a young man from Materfi had eloped with a girl from Al-Shaqiq, after a rebellious and emotional love affair. The scandal was devastating, and each village blamed the other. Things escalated when the people of Al-Shaqiq suddenly attacked the Materfi village to take revenge for the shame and disgrace they felt had been caused. They killed and injured some Materfi residents, then retreated. A short time later, the Materfi sought vengeance, and the tit-for-tat skirmishes carried on for a long time until the elders from both villages agreed to stop the bloodshed and avoid meetings in any way.

Awad was the cousin of the young man who eloped with the girl. Two of his brothers had been killed by the people of Al-Shaqiq in one of the rounds of violence. We used to know each other, but now we never met face-to-face. Venom and malice were filling his eyes while he looked at us on the edge of the spring.

"What do you want, Awad? We are here to swim."

Hearing my question, Awad let out a harsh laugh. He was the same age as we were, but he was much bigger, tougher and more arrogant. He folded his arms behind his back and walked to the edge of the spring.

"All right, let me explain what I see," he said. "Two persons of the same age, sitting next to each other in an isolated place near a spring. There is nobody around, they are both naked, but what hides the shameful thing we were about to see. What were we about to see, guys?

Awad directed the question to his three friends who burst into laughter, enjoying the sport. They were similar in age and united by lust for violence, revenge, and readiness to get involved in a fight of any kind. Ghassan's face grew red with rage. I shouted at Awad, trying to avoid a scuffle.

"Please, Awad, we don't want to get into the spiral of problems again. We have had enough of them in the past, you know that."

"What are you doing here, near this spring? Don't you know that it is located within the boundaries of our village, stupid boys?," Awad said angrily, while looking us in the eyes trying to provoke our anger.

Ghassan spoke up.

"No, it is not within the boundaries of your village. You know it is in the middle area between the two villages, and it is the only area that was not annexed to either village so that everyone could get the benefit from it."

"Do you hear who is speaking?"

The beefy guy put his hand beside his ear in a theatrical way, as if he found it difficult to hear Ghassan's voice. He turned to his friends, scratching his rough, curly hair and then spoke to my friend again.

"You are the son of that date trader, aren't you? Have they finally taught you the art of speaking? I'm sure they regretted that when they heard your feminine voice."

"Awad!,"Ghassan screamed, his anger exploding.

His chest started to heave up and down out of rage. I held his arm trying to calm him down, but it seemed that Awad was enjoying himself too much, so he took some steps towards us and leaned his body towards Ghassan.

"Oh, my God! Look at the delicate, fair complexion this cutie has!," he mocked.

He took further steps towards us, all the while trying to humiliate Ghassan, until he was very close to his face. Ghassan did not blink. Awad gave a sinister smile, exposing ugly, yellow teeth and looked Ghassan up and down.

"If this is what their son looks like, I can't stop myself from imagining his sister!" he jeered.

At that exact moment, I realised that things were out of control. Ghassan punched Awad in the face and he moved back, forced by the blow and the shock. I knew then that things were not going to end well.

In a flash, I gathered a handful of sand from beside the water and threw it in the eyes of Awad's gang, who had dashed to support their leader. They screamed, as they flailed around, fumbling to get the dirt out of their eyes. One of them rushed towards me holding a piece of tree trunk and hit me on the shoulder. I screamed out in pain. Awad jumped to his feet, his eyes flaming in fury. Ghassan knew that striking the first blow was the only advantage he had. That element of surprise had now gone.

He ran away to the tall, thick palm trees that pierced the sky. Awad ran after him until they both reached the fence that surrounded the spring. Ghassan was trapped and tried to jump into the spring but before he made it, Awad caught up with him, threw him to the ground and sat on him, beating him hard.

Ghassan lay helplessly under Awad's big heavy frame, but eventually managed to wriggle free and flee towards the water. He climbed over a large metal pipe that was covered with slippery algae, then jumped into the spring.

Awad rushed after him, roaring in anger. He also tried to climb over the pipe, but slipped on the algae. His chubby body twisted in the air for a moment then he fell on his head in the water.

Ghassan got out of the water quickly and with a trembling hand, picked up a piece of tree trunk from the ground, waiting for Awad to get out of the water. Everybody was silent, the friends and the enemies, the war had abated all of a sudden and all those who were involved in it were looking at each other, not sure what to do next. My friend looked at me with questioning eyes, the piece of trunk shaking in his hand as his whole body trembled.

Chapter 7

The house was in a state of alert. The doors were wide open, and everyone was searching from room to room. . Fear was rife but the idea was too strange to believe. How could a mother vanish in this way?

Jalal paced back and forth in the sitting room, overwhelmed with worry. He was the first one to discover she was gone. He had woken up downstairs in the sitting room to the sound of the call to prayer coming from his mobile.

He walked up to their bedroom but did not find his wife sleeping in her bed as he expected. He thought she might be still angry about what had happened the night before, and so had chosen to sleep in one of the children's bedrooms instead. When he came back after prayers, he went looking for her in every room of the house, wanting to apologise. He searched the kitchen, the bathrooms, the outer section of the house, before he finally realised she was not there.

Khatir sat next to his elder sister, who had hurried to the house with her husband as soon as she heard what had happened. Sara cried when she saw Khatir crying , he was so afraid and seemed not to understand what was going on. They were all sleepy and in a state of shock, but Khatir appeared to be struggling the most. All he wanted at that moment was to see his mother in front of him.

Jalal's neighbour Khalifa entered the house. He was not wearing his headdress and he was still buttoning his jalabiya, his eyes still watery with sleep behind his thick rectangular glasses. Jalal welcomed the police detective quickly, hoping he might have immediate answers as to the whereabouts of his wife. But he knew nothing more than they did.

"I'm doing my best, but such cases cannot be solved this way, especially at this early hour. We have to go to the police station and report her absence."

"The police station?," Jalal burst in. "Do you want to create a scandal? And let all people far and wide talk about us, Khalifa? I called you because you have a lot of experience in this field and because I don't want this news to fly around. We have lived in the same neighbourhood since you moved here many years ago, and you must help us without going to the police station. Please, my son."

Khalifa touched his bald head in bemusement. The age gap between them was not that big, but Jalal always considered him as a son. Ali joined in the conversation, folding his arms on his chest.

"What can be done in such cases?," he asked.

Khalifa let out a deep sigh before asking them all to sit down and retell the details of what had happened the night before. Jalal told him about the party and Ghassan's visit. Khalifa scratched his wide chin.

"So it was a terrible night for all of you," he murmured. "Did you check her things? Clothes? Belongings? Is anything missing? Did you lose anything from the house?"

"Everything in the house is in its place. The only thing that is missing is her," Jalal said.

"How many exits are there from this house? It seems to me to be a vast building," Khalifa asked, scanning the house with his eyes, sounding professional.

"There are two external gates - the first is the one you used to come inside the house and the second is at the back where you can come and go from the other side," answered Jalal. "And yes, the house has three floors, in the middle of the stairs, the floor is split into two parts. One part leads to the hall here, and the other leads to the other part of the house, which includes the front courtyard. Here you can see the palm trees. At the back of the house there is nothing apart from rickety old stuff, a worn-out wardrobe and an old water tank."

"Why don't you get rid of all that rubbish if you don't use any of it?" Khalifa asked.

"I'm thinking of that because these things are blocking the way and they look hideous. But Lameya won't let me get rid of the wardrobe. As for the water tank, Khatir uses it as a hideout. He spends a lot of his time there, so his mother furnished it and moved his toys there. Sometimes, she joins him there."

"Did you check the back door?"

"If you are suggesting that she left the house because of what happened last night, I can assure you that Lameya wouldn't do something like that," Jalal said sharply.

"We have had many conflicts during our long years together, but she has never thought of leaving the house or departing in this way. I know my wife very well."

Khalifa nodded and raised his hands.

"I am not saying she has left you, but there is a possibility that she was feeling very distressed and aggrieved last night. So perhaps she decided to go to the house of one of her relatives or to a friend. Maybe she wanted you to feel guilty about what happened!"

"How can going to stay with a relative or a friend be a possibility when she didn't take anything with her? She can't have done that!"

Jalal's voice was rising, mind refusing to accept the idea. Khalifa could not argue back, so Ali stepped in with his professional perspective.

'I do agree with my uncle, Khalifa. My aunt Lameya is not the sort of person who would do such a thing. Her wisdom and common sense would stop her from leaving like this. Her family is her utmost priority, so it does not make any sense that after all these years, she would leave in this mysterious way."

The room fell silent. Everyone looked gloomy and

distressed, grief and puzzlement dominating the scene. Jalal murmured in sorrow, as if he were talking to himself.

"What makes me afraid is her medicine. She knows that she has to take her drugs regularly. That is another cause against your argument, Khalifa."

"What medicine?"

Grief clouded Jalal's eyes as he started to explain his wife's chronic medical condition.

"She has had heart failure since her childhood, and this causes her ongoing troubles as well as acute pain in the chest area. It gets worse when she exerts herself, does sports or exercise, sometimes even lying in bed. I have woken up scared at night many times having found her covered in sweat and struggling to catch her breath."

Khatir was sitting restlessly beside his sister, his distress growing all the time.

"I want my mother, I want my mother. Please, bring her now," he screamed, bursting into tears. His sister pulled him into her arms, trying to reassure herself as well as him.

"Don't worry, my dear, we will find her and everything will be alright. Don't cry, please."

Khalifa lowered his head, affected by the tragic scene of the family. His face darkened, and he spoke with the seriousness of someone in his profession. "If she did not leave of her own free will, then this means that she was forced to leave. In other words, she was kidnapped."

A shudder swept through all of them, for it was a dreadful possibility to consider their mother being taken by force and held against her will. Khalifa scanned the eyes of the people around him and took a deep breath.

"Now, tell me, who do you think has the motive to do such a thing?," he said, cautiously.

Silence. They exchanged perplexed looks between them. Lameya had no enemies, and they could think of no-one who could hate her nor anything that would justify an act of kidnapping. She was a peaceful dove, always helping others in their worst moments, never doing any harm.

She had such emotional intelligence she could forge deep relationships with others. The possibility that anyone could hate or hurt their mother in this way was not an option at all. Everyone respected her and loved her.

Jalal broke the silence with a weak moan.

"Ghassan!"

Chapter 8

The crowds dispersed after Friday prayers in the only mosque in the village. In the outer corner, I was standing in a shaded spot to avoid sunstroke.

It was the middle of the Holy month of Ramadan. My throat was dry. It was only early afternoon but I felt thirsty already. I had waited for a long time for my friend Ghassan to come out of the mosque with the Sudanese Sheikh Othman, who used to call for prayers in the mosque and lead prayers when the Imam was absent. He also supervised Holy Quran reading circle, which my friend had regularly taken part in for many years.

That had created a special bond between Ghassan and Sheikh Othman and they used to speak about many topics related to the Holy Quran such as Hadith (sayings of the Prophet), the nation's uprising and evil deeds. They also used to talk about the need for constancy and adherence to the principles and values of Islam.

When Ghassan said farewell to Sheikh Othman, he approached me and apologised for being late. I chastised him for keeping me waiting.

"What were you discussing this time? Could you not have postponed it?"

"I will tell you everything on our way home. Let's go."

As we usually did every Friday, we stopped at the grocery store near the mosque. We had known its owner, Hamdi, since our early childhood. Later on, his sons would sell the grocery shop to someone who would turn it into a shoe shop.

Each of us bought things that our families had asked us to bring for the Ramadan breakfast, as well as our favourite drink to have when Magrib Azan is called at mosque (It is a signal of the end of fasting period during the Holy month of Ramadan at time of sunset).

We walked off towards home under the burning sun.

"Have you seen anyone from the Materfi village after that accident?," Ghassan asked.

"No, I haven't. Please, don't get us involved in any more troubles. We only just managed to escape that situation, which almost led to war again between the two villages. We were only free of it when the comrades of Awad testified that we had nothing to do with his death."

Ghassan stayed silent for a couple of moments, then drew a deep breath as if he were about to disclose a serious secret.

"I intend to get married."

"Get married? Are you serious?"

I turned to him in astonishment. But he was completely calm.

"Yes, I am serious. Why not? My future employment at Aramco is confirmed now and they will give me a very good salary. Also, my name was enlisted in their scholarship programme to study abroad. I'm doing my best to join it because it will give me additional privileges at work and an increase in the salary I earn now."

"But where are you going to live?"

"My father will allocate a part of the house to us to live in until I can settle in a separate house afterwards."

We walked in silence for a while.

"Don't you think that it is too early for that?," I exclaimed.

"We are no longer young, Jalal. I'm 22 years old now and you are over 20. My father and your father got married at a very early age. And besides, all the details have already been facilitated and coordinated."

"Don't tell me that you have already chosen your bride?"

I stopped walking and grabbed his shoulder. He laughed.

"What do you think made me think about getting married,

then?" he said. "Yes, I have chosen one and talked to my mother about her. I was talking just now to Sheikh Othman about my intentions of getting married and he encouraged me to do so."

We resumed our walk, but the questions kept coming.

"Which house will be doomed and punished by destiny for you choosing their daughter?," I said in jest.

Ghassan stopped and pointed to a house that had been recently renovated and seemed rich and luxurious. It was behind the Stars Sports Club that we used to play in as children. I shouted in surprise.

"The house of Mr. Saleh?"

He smiled shyly and nodded his head in confirmation.

"He was one of the best teachers who taught us, but I don't remember him having a daughter that could be at the age to get married," I said. "I only remember his son who drowned a while ago. Everyone felt sad about that dreadful accident, God bless his soul."

"He has a daughter. She looks young, but she is old enough to get married and when I asked my mother about her age, she said she was about 17 years old."

He blushed when he mentioned her.

"So, you have planned for everything, cunning guy?" I teased. "Alright, all I can say is that I pray for God to grant you the best of luck, my friend."

He did not respond, he just gave me a smile revealing the passion and the delight that was filling his heart. Then he asked a question in an attempt to change the course of the conversation.

"Will you come over to our house tonight to watch TV?

"Do you think I will miss Sheikh Tantawi's lecture?"

Three weeks after this talk, on a Friday after the evening prayers at the house of Mr Saleh and in the presence of considerable people in the village, including my father and my uncles, Ghassan was officially engaged.

That was the day I saw Lameya for the first time.

Glittering coloured ribbons were dangling from the walls of Mr Saleh's house and at the front, they had put up a tent on three poles. Guests were seated in the different corners, filled with the joy of Eid as well as the forthcoming marriage. In the middle sat the Sheikh and on his right sat Mr Saleh, while my friend Ghassan was seated on the left. He was elegantly dressed, but that elegance could not hide his awkwardness. He was playing anxiously with a yellow rosary, a nervous smile lingering on his face.

I was moving in and out of the tent, back and forth, carrying cups of coffee for washing and roaming with the fragrant incense. Every now and then I went into the courtyard of Mr Saleh's house, which was the centre for the women's celebrations. It was the source of much clapping and calls to bring what the men needed, such as cups of coffee, plates of dates and fruits. I felt delighted for Ghassan and was sharing his joy and happiness.

When the marriage agreement was officially concluded, I

hugged my friend tight and congratulated him. Then my father gestured to me to bring dinner, so I carried the large plate of fruits and then dashed towards the courtyard, where I came across a group of women including my sister. They were leaving the outside room, heading inside and among them, a young woman was walking slowly, her head lowered in shyness. She was wearing a transparent white veil on her head and was holding it in place with her hand, which was decorated with henna.

When I came inside at exactly the same time, all eyes in the group were focused on me with surprise and condemnation. The first one of them was my sister, who gestured to me angrily. The whole situation only lasted a few seconds but it was like touching a burning matchstick - it only takes a moment but leaves a lasting impact.

My sister scolded me, and I lost my balance, dropping the plate of fruit and causing a tremendous crash, with all the things on the plate scattering on the ground. I was highly embarrassed. From their perspective, I was not only an intruder but had also spoiled their party. I had been caught red-handed. I turned in awkwardness and closed the door behind me while my heart was trembling violently.

Later that night when all the guests had left, I stayed with Ghassan, his father, and some of their relatives. I was exhausted, so I threw my tired body next to him.

"You owe me a lot, my friend," I sighed with relief. "You were here celebrating and enjoying your time, while I was running here and there, doing difficult tasks."

He giggled then threw a piece of banana left over from the dinner towards me.

"Come on and find yourself a bride as I have done," he said. "And I will celebrate your marriage as no one ever did. I will dance as well. You are a true brother, Jalal, and I will never forget your favour."

His father jumped into the conversation after patting my shoulder tenderly, as he often did.

"I have always considered you as my son, Jalal, since you

and Ghassan played together in the courtyard of our house. At that time, I realised that God had gifted me with another son as well as mine. I'm so proud of you."

An hour later, we were back at home. I was sitting in the living room and everyone was chatting about the engagement party - all its fine details, the quality of the food, joyous comments here and there. I bent my head toward my sister.

"It was an embarrassing situation, wasn't it?," I whispered.

My sister looked at me angrily.

"Are you crazy? You froze in your place instead of hurrying out as you should have done. What happened to you?"

"I didn't see anything, I swear. It was just a quick glance!"

I looked aside and stayed silent with a smile on my face. I was remembering the details of the night. When my sister went to her room, I followed her and asked,

"Who was the girl who was covering her face with the transparent white veil?"

"A quick glance, ha?"

She looked at me with suspicion that seemed to see right through me.

"Are you telling me or not?," I asked again.

"She is Lameya, your friend's wife."

I spent my whole night awake in my bed staring at the space in the room. My eyes refused to close and rest. In that moment, I knew for sure that things must not go as they had been planned.

Chapter 9

Khalifa took out his mobile phone and played with the buttons as he hesitated, while Jalal pleaded with him in desperation.

"Please, Khalifa, believe me. Ghassan is the one who did it, believe me. I am sure of that, my son."

The situation in the house had reached a climax. Tensions and distress were stiffening the air. Jalal was unshakable in his belief that his former friend turned enemy was behind all of this.

The other family members, however, were not so sure. They all agreed that the events of the previous night had been difficult and painful, and that things spiralled out of control. But they weren't convinced it meant Ghassan had kidnapped Lameya.

"This is out of my hands. How can I bring someone here without permission and without an official record? That would be an explicit violation of the law and would make me the subject of an internal investigation," Khalifa tried to explain.

"Please, Khalifa, I have told you before about all those formal regulations and the police. There is no time for doing that now. He told me that he is staying at the Intercontinental Hotel and that his plane is leaving at eight this morning. Please just bring him here."

Jalal swallowed bitterly.

"Of course, if he is still in the hotel and has not already escaped"

He jumped up from his seat. He remembered that he had Ghassan's number saved on his mobile after they had exchanged contact details yesterday afternoon. He hurried upstairs to get it, disappearing for a few moments before coming back with heavy footsteps and a shocked expression on his face. He was holding a small piece of paper in his hand, eyes focused on it as he walked towards them.

"Uncle! What's wrong?" asked Ali.

Jalal did not answer, but handed the piece of paper to Khalifa with trembling hands. Ali stood beside him, craning his neck to read what was on it.

It had been typed with the words,

I swear that you will not be blessed from now on. You don't deserve her; you don't deserve her.

"Where did you get it? Who gave it to you?," Khalifa demanded

"I went to look for my mobile and I found it there on my desk. I didn't notice it before, only now!," wailed Jalal.

He got closer to Khalifa and squeezed his hand hard.

"Are you convinced now? Are you?" Jalal's voice trembled. "They are the same words and the same threat Ghassan articulated last night!"

Khalifa took a deep breath. He was fully aware of how serious the situation was becoming, and how serious it would be when his line managers discovered what he was doing. He hesitantly pressed some buttons on his mobile and then made up his mind to make a call.

"Hello! Can you do me a favour?"

A whole minute passed before Khalifa got approval from the man on the other side. They agreed on sending the full name, address and all of Ghassan's personal details. He ended the call and placed his mobile on the table in front of him.

"Someone is on their way to him," he said in a serious, police tone. "He is one of my friends who works as a detective. He will use his official authority to bring him here."

Jalal shook his knee.

"I will tear him up with those hands!"

"Please, uncle, we still don't have decisive evidence," Ali said in an objective way. He was trying to avoid the trap of overrunning emotions, but his father-in-law screamed at him in rage.

'We don't have evidence? Didn't you hear him last night? He threatened me explicitly. He said he will deprive me of her and will make me taste pain and deprivation! And what about this piece of paper? I have been calling his number for half an hour, but his mobile is shut off. Aren't all these shreds of evidence?

Ali lowered his head in embarrassment. He did not want to argue with his father-in-law who seemed ready to explode in the face of everyone and could create a fight at any moment, even with his own family members.

"Please, dad!," pleaded Sara. "Calm down, my husband just wanted to help!"

Khalifa's phone rang, interrupting the tense family stand-off. Khalifa picked it up, while everyone listened in for news. After a few minutes, he closed the mobile.

"Ghassan is not in the hotel," he said in a low voice.

"What does that mean, Khalifa?"

"My friend said that when he asked at the reception, they informed him that he had checked out half an hour ago. He had taken his bags and all his belongings, and left the hotel."

Jalal slammed the table in front of him with his fist.

"The cursed man ran away. I told you I'm not mistaken, but you didn't listen to me," he roared. "If you had done what I told you earlier instead of babbling, we would have managed to catch him."

"What are we going to do now?" said Ali in a desperate and helpless voice. Jalal put his hands on his head in pity and confusion and started to walk up and down the hall, back and forth.

No-one said a word, and the silence was suffocating. Khatir was biting his nails as he always did when he was anxious. His eyes were still wet with tears. "Where could he have gone?" Khalifa asked.

Nobody had an answer. But what Jalal was thinking made

his head and heart ache. "If I did something as bad as this and was afraid of being discovered, I would head for the nearest airport."

He let out a short scream then he picked up his mobile and with trembling fingers, he pressed some buttons.

"The airport, he must be at the airport now," he mumbled. "The plane should not fly taking that bastard onboard."

"What are you going to do?,"Khalifa asked, but Jalal ignored him. He was focusing on the screen of his mobile, searching for a particular number. He pressed the dial button then put it on speaker so they all could hear the sound. He placed the mobile on the table when someone answered.

"Hello, Adel, this is Jalal. I need urgent help from you right now."

"Do you know what time it is?"

Adel's voice came heavy and sleepy, he yawned audibly and then mumbled some prayers. Jalal pressed on.

"Please Adel. You are the only one who can help me at the airport."

"Help? What kind of help do you want?"

"I want to know if a person has left or not. His flight is scheduled to leave very soon and I need to stop him from travelling at once."

The speaker could be heard shuffling around in his bed.

"Jalal, you are my friend, my neighbour, and I very much like you," Adel said, in a serious tone. "But I cannot do that. This information is very confidential, and we cannot disclose it. In addition, it's the weekend, I'm not on duty and I'm sleeping in my bed right now. If you look at your watch, my words will make sense to you!"

"Please, Adel, do me this favour and I will never forget it. There isn't any time to waste."

A moment of silence and then...

"Alright, I will see what I can do."

Jalal shut his mobile in relief, then they all waited with

baited breath. Khatir was still weeping beside his sister. Then the mobile rang again. Jalal picked it up quickly and pressed the speaker.

"Adel, you took your time. What happened?"

They all listened to the sound of fingers quickly clicking a keyboard on the other side of the line. Then Adel said, his mouth full,

"The connection sucks here. I will report this to the damned company until they wish they had never launched it. Tell me, Jalal, what is the name of your internet provider, do you recommend it?"

"Adel, we don't have much time. Just tell me, has that plane taken off or not yet?"

Jalal was impatient and had no patience for Adel's chit chat. Adel gulped down a drink.

"Here we are, my dear, let's see," he said, slowly. "Now, let's insert the name of the passenger you gave me so that the number of the flight he booked appears,"

"Adel! Just get on with it!"

Adel clicked the keyboard.

"Alright, alright, we can say that the plane took off seven minutes ago."

Jalal's face darkened. He knew this was a likely outcome, but his mind did not want to accept that everything was over.

"Nothing can be done now. Lameya has gone forever."

He threw his body on the sofa in desperation.

"But.."

Adel kept talking.

"Ghassan was not on board."

Jalal jumped to his feet again and moved close to the mobile on the table.

"What do you mean, he is still here?"

Just then, there was a knock at the door. They all looked at each other. This was not an appropriate time for receiving guests of any sort. The family was in crisis and nerves had been on the edge since dawn.

"Anybody here?"

Everyone gasped. The knocking was coming from the interior door, not from the outside gate. The door opened a little bit and a man appeared from the other side, the very last person they expected to see. They never thought that Ghassan would come back into the house of his own accord.

Chapter 10

One Wednesday afternoon, about a month after the engagement, I was at the Stars Club kicking a ball around, dressed in my green national sports tracksuit. The colour had faded by now, and the fabric was thinning because of excessive use and frequent washing. The sun was focusing its rays on my head without mercy and hot drops of sweat were dripping from my thick hair.

The beeping of a car horn from outside the club interrupted me. I ignored it at first and went on kicking the ball, but the horn came again, more insistently this time. I picked up the ball and went out of the club, and was astounded to see pulled up outside a fancy ivory-coloured car with elegant red lines stretching along its long, graceful body. It was enchanting and its round headlights captivated the mind.

I felt my jaw drop. And then Ghassan got out of the car. He was on cloud nine, overwhelmed with excitement.

"I knew I would find you here when I went by your house and you weren't there. What do you think?"

He touched the soft ceiling of the car. I was struck dumb and could not say a word. I just stared.

"Gosh! How lovely!," I finally managed to say.

"Not only that."

He signalled to me to get inside the car. I opened the door cautiously and was welcomed by the scent of the hot leather seats. He settled next to me and then closed the doors. He pressed a button on the dashboard and the car was instantly filled with the voice of Talal Al-Maddah, singing,

"Oh, my friend, love gives no comfort!

Beware, don't sell your heart to those who hurt it."

Ghassan was waiting for my response and my face flooded with happiness. For me, it was a magic formula - a new brand of Nissan cars combined with the warm sound of my favourite singer. I will not hesitate to say that this was my ultimate dream.

"I didn't know that you liked listening to him!," I said, regaining my composure.

He turned down the sound, then turned to me.

"You know, I don't like listening to songs, but I know how much you love him and I know he can make you happy," he said, "so I borrowed this tape from my father to complete the surprise."

I felt both gratitude and envy all at once. He turned the steering wheel, and the car ran swiftly over the ground. When it reached the asphalt road, the car went off gracefully. We passed the big house of Mr Saleh and I articulated a thought that had been haunting me for a while.

"I have no idea how the teacher Saleh became that rich! I still remember his old rickety house and his worn-out clothes. Did he find a spring that flows with gold?"

"That spring flowed in every house here," Ghassan said as we drove by. "Blessings spread and reached all people. When King Khalid returned from having treatment for his knee, he gave orders to increase the salaries of all the employees. It was almost an 80 per cent increase. I heard my father saying that each palm tree and each goat would even have a salary due to the overwhelming blessing."

"I'm not surprised that your father's philosophy is based on dates and palm trees!," I joked.

Ghassan ignored my comment and turned into the road that led outside the village.

"The teachers, in particular, were paid generously. Two years ago, their salaries were increased. As well as that, he gave them a 50,000 riyals allowance and a piece of land as a grant for every new teacher. Last Ramadan, he also gave everyone two months' worth of salary to all employees in the kingdom. Not only that, he granted 25,000 riyals for every teacher who had completed 25 years of service. Mr Saleh got the maximum benefit from these grants, so he launched his own company. That is what has earned him so much money."

We drove on a rural road lined with palm trees on both sides.

"So that explains why he gave his consent for you to marry his daughter. You all eat with golden spoons, unlike us," I said sarcastically.

He slowed the car gradually until it came to a complete stop, letting a herd of sheep and a shepherd with a stick cross the road. After the dust cloud made by the animals died down, he drove on. A question was stuck inside my throat, but I could not keep it quiet for long, so I asked while I was looking through the glass at the palm trees beside the road.

"Did you agree on the wedding date?"

I swallowed with difficulty while waiting for Ghassan to respond. He was scratching his beard and thinking.

"We haven't talked about that yet, but I don't want to wait too long. I may get approval to complete my postgraduate study abroad any time now."

I choked and felt bitter heaviness in my heart. Talal was still singing inside the car, but I could not make any sense of his words.

"I'm not sure if that is appropriate for her or will endanger her," Ghassan whispered after a few seconds of silence.

"What do you mean?" I looked towards him, confused.

"She suffers from heart defects along with difficulties in breathing and other symptoms."

He seemed distressed.

"She needs specialist health care and intensive check-ups to make sure she takes her medicines. These mitigate the symptoms and to stop her condition from being aggravated. Any negligence in any way will make her heart completely stop."

His eyes glistened with tears and he looked aside towards the window.

Then he drew a deep breath.

"When I was at their house the last time, I felt sure that I was doing the right thing. I knew about her sickness before we got engaged and I will never regret choosing her as a wife. I just wish I could replace her ill heart with mine, because I can't bear to ever see her in pain."

My heart was beating fast with every sentence that his trembling lips were uttering. I looked at him in silence. I did not know what I should say, for everything seemed wrong from my point of view. All the lovely things should not go to one person while the others are left with nothing. It seemed completely unfair from my perspective. Riches, success and family should be divided among people equally. It is not my fault that my father was needy and indigent. I also had ambitions to have a good salary waiting for me at the end of each month.

This is not fair, I thought. I had to take action. I could not
allow this to happen. I must not lose everything.

I leaned my head against the glass of the window and
looked out at the sea of palm trees that was racing past in
front of my eyes, the sound of Talal sneaking into my ears
like warm liquid gold.

"He is poor who thinks that love is heaven

After two days he will be disappointed,

and will say love brings no comfort."

Oh, my friend."

Chapter 11

Before they could process what was going on, Jalal dashed towards the door grabbing Ghassan by his clothes. Ghassan was startled, for he was not ready for the sudden attack. Jalal dragged him inside the room and Ghassan stumbled on the leg of the table and was about to fall. Khalifa and Ali hurried towards them, pulling each one to a separate corner.

The intruder stood breathless, struggling to regain his balance. Khalifa was standing in front of him and on the other side, Jalal was erupting in rage, cursing and shouting abusive language, trying to free himself from his son-in-law who had him trapped between his arms in an attempt to control him.

"How dare you come here, bastard? I swear I will bury you alive."

Khalifa tried to impose control over the situation using a stern, military voice.

"That's enough! Do you want your wife to come back or not? If you carry on like this, you won't ever see her again."

Jalal swallowed his tongue, eyes still fixed on Ghassan, but he started to regain control of himself. His breathing settled as he accepted the issue could be solved with fists.

"What are you talking about? Be sure that I haven't come here to see your ugly face again," Ghassan said, while tidying his clothes after the storm of violence that had come at him out of the blue.

Jalal waved an admonishing finger at him.

"What are we talking about?" he shouted. "Are you going to act the role of the idiot now? By the way, it is the most suitable role for you to act. Ghassan! Tell us now! Where is Lameya?"

"Lameya?," asked Ghassan. "What's wrong with her?"

Before Jalal could explode again, Ali asked his wife and Khatir to move to the other sitting room on the opposite side of the hall. Khalifa asked the rest to sit down to begin a sensible discussion about the situation.

"Lameya, the wife of this man, is missing. She hasn't been seen since the dawn of this day," Khalifa said with authority.

"The only jerk who could have done such a thing is definitely you!" screamed Jalal, before Khalifa signalled to him to stay silent and control himself.

Ghassan waited for a few seconds.

"I'm sorry to hear that, but I have nothing to do with it," he said.

"What made you come here this morning after what happened last night?" Khalifa asked sternly.

"I lost my mobile. I looked for it everywhere and the last time I remember having it was in this place. All my work stuff and files are uploaded on it, so it is important. I thought I might have lost it in this house when this villain pushed me and made me drop my glasses."

"So that's why your mobile has been off all the time?" Khalifa said, raising his eyebrows at Jalal for jumping to conclusions and rushing to accuse Ghassan.

Ghassan continued.

"I missed my flight to come here and find it. I found all the doors of the house were wide open. I was surprised. I stepped in, trying to see if anyone was home. Then this maniac pulled me inside!"

"This maniac will kick your throat until you throw up your blood if you don't tell us where Lameya is," said Jalal, threatening Ghassan with a clenched fist.

Ghassan shrugged his shoulders.

"How on earth would I know where she is?" he exclaimed.

Khalifa took on a more professional approach.

"We think that you have kidnapped her to take revenge on

Jalal for the long history you both have, and because of what happened last night. It might be some sort of mad response from you about all of that," he said.

Ghassan's eyes nearly popped out of the sockets behind his round glasses. He scanned the faces of everyone in the room to make sure they were being serious.

"You are kidding me, aren't you? This is nonsense! How dare you accuse me of such a deed? I'm not obliged to stay here. If you have family issues, manage it yourselves and don't involve me."

He jumped to his feet to leave, but his opponent's threatening voice thundered again.

"Oh, do you really want to go to the police station? That would be so much fun, especially when they know that you were in my house the night before my wife disappeared and that you threatened to make me taste pain and deprivation. We all heard that. We are all witnesses, especially after I found this piece of paper! There is no way you can deny what you did, eloquent buddy!"

All the eyes were on Ghassan, who looked utterly perplexed. He took the piece of paper that Jalal threw at him and passed his eyes over the words while struggling to swallow.

"Did that actually happen? Did you threaten him?," asked Khalifa.

He blinked, feeling anxiety and embarrassment.

"Yes, I did say that, but I did not really mean it. And anyway, I have absolutely nothing to do with this piece of paper."

"Are you aware that threatening people is a violation of the law and you could be punished consequently?" said Khalifa, in a loud stern tone.

"But I didn't do anything, do you understand? It is true that I was overwhelmed with rage and was not thinking of what I was saying as all people do when they are furious. The words came out in the course of my speech just to frighten him and show him how angry I was, but I never meant it!"

"You are lying!" Jalal shouted.

"I swear I didn't do it! How can I get into a house and kidnap a person without anyone knowing? How can you be snatched from your room and not make any fuss?"

A pause before Khalifa spoke.

"We don't know how you did it, we only know that you did it. We know that you came to this house, had a quarrel with its owner and ended it with threats and intimidation. You said that you would deprive him as he did to you. As an experienced investigator, I suggest that you confess and disclose her place immediately, Ghassan. All the evidence points to you."

"I swear I didn't do it," protested Ghassan. "A man my age cannot do that. How can I do such a thing?"

"Oh yes, it is very possible," said Jalal, who had stood up again in anger. His son-in-law jumped up too and stood in front of him.

"Because you are a mean, worthless scoundrel," Jalal shouted over Ali's shoulder. "Confess now, where did you hide her? Tell us or you will regret it, you bastard!"

Ghassan opened his mouth and jumped up from his seat.

"Enough is enough, you villain! I cannot put up with you anymore. If you had been a real man, you would have managed your family and wife. But you keep proving your failure and ignorance."

Chaos ensued, with curses and insults flying once more. Khalifa parted them again.

"Stop it now!" he admonished. "Or else I will have to take you both to the police station. Being here is against the rules and regulations, so don't force me to do something you will all regret. Do you understand what I'm saying?"

Both opponents felt the seriousness of the situation and there was a spontaneous silent truce. They sat down while Khalifa remained standing, watching the impact of his words on them. Ali went to find his wife.

Chapter 12

Silence fell over the place while the two opponents exchanged hostile looks. Meanwhile, Khalifa sat in the middle between them. He was stumped by this strange case. He didn't like the accusation laid against Ghassan right from the beginning; the difficulty of breaking into the house and kidnapping the wife made it difficult for him to believe Jalal's claims.

A few moments passed, then Ali appeared once again with Sara behind him. She was supporting her back with her hand and had placed the other on her swollen belly. She was wrapped in a black abaya and her face was covered with a transparent veil. The sun rays sneaking from the open door were falling on her face. The rustle of the palm trees swaying in the courtyard was soothing. Khatir followed her, his face red, and he sat in the corner of the sitting room.

Khalifa took off his thick glasses and rubbed the corner of his eyes.

"I want to post some questions to you and I want to hear all the details about what happened last night. Tell me everything and don't forget the fine details, even if you think they are trivial. Everything can help us find your mother as soon as possible."

Sara looked at her husband and her father, choked back her tears and then spoke with a shaky voice. She told him everything she had witnessed, starting from the moment she arrived at the anniversary party until the arrival of the stranger and the quarrel that had happened. Ghassan lowered his head in awkwardness when those embarrassing details were mentioned. Meanwhile, his opponent was shaking his leg nervously and impatiently.

Sara went on to describe the flow of actions in detail and reached the part where her parents had quarrelled. She told him about the painful slap on the face and at that moment, Khalifa stopped her and asked her to confirm what she had just said.

"You say that your father slapped your mother on the face after a big quarrel?"

"Yes, that was very painful for all of us."

"How did your mother respond afterwards?" Khalifa asked.

Sara lowered her head when she recalled that scene.

"She was really shocked. I have never seen my parents reach that point before.

She was angry and said that her father was not mistaken when he had warned her about giving her money to my father. Then, she said that it was not over yet."

Everyone looked at Jalal then, who was reeling with

embarrassment. Ghassan let out a sarcastic laugh.

"That's it then! And you ask me why your wife disappeared?"

Khalifa signalled to him to be quiet. Then he turned to Jalal.

"Did that really happen, Jalal?"

Jalal's hands were shaking, he was in a state of aggravated anxiety. He began to stutter an answer.

"Yes, that's right. We were all very angry and I could not control myself, unfortunately. I was forced to do that when she irritated me."

"But you haven't mentioned anything about this before!" Khalifa had raised his voice.

Before Jalal answered, Ghassan crossed his legs, scratched his beard, and gloated.

"What are you waiting for him to say, Mr Policeman? Do you want him to tell you that he was scared after she threatened him? Or do you want him to tell you that he could not sleep last night, because he was thinking of how to get out of the trap he created from his stupidity?"

Ghassan's tone turned very cold, stern and laden with hatred. Stressing every word, he focused on his opponent's eyes.

"Or do you want him to admit that he planned all of this so he could keep all her money before she took any steps to destroy his greedy efforts?"

Jalal widened his eyes. Everyone was full of suspicions, including Khalifa. He was startled by the way the whole scene was being turned upside down. Ghassan had done it in such a skillful way! Jalal sensed the growing suspicions of all the people in the room. Despite their silence, their looks were sharp, reflecting what they were thinking inside. He swallowed, and then spoke with a sound he struggled to make stable.

"What is this nonsense you are raving about? Are you crazy?"

He looked at the others who were staring at him.

"This is nonsense!" he said, defensively. "He is trying to shift the accusation to me. You all know how much I love my wife and there is no reason whatsoever that would make me hurt her."

"What about her father's money?" Khalifa interrupted him. He was not being sympathetic with him at that moment. Jalal kept silent for a few seconds, trying to organise his thoughts.

"That happened many years ago. When her father died, we had been married for years. He left a fortune and his only daughter, Lameya, inherited it all when her mother died. She gave me power of attorney to manage all her money and property. I invested the money in a very fruitful way and managed to double the money and multiply it. She used to say that her father was mistaken when he advised her not to give all her money to me, but.."

"But now, after all these years, you are proving that Mr Saleh was right. How cunning you are!"

Ghassan interrupted him with eyes filled with disgust, but Jalal continued to defend himself.

"I didn't do anything! How can I hurt my wife, the mother of my children, after all these long years of marriage?"

He turned to his daughter who was trying to process what she heard.

"Please, daughter, don't listen to these lies!," he pleaded. "You know that I cannot do anything that harms your mother, do you understand this?"

Sara did not answer. The situation was logical and made sense when the charge was pointing towards Ghassan, and all the evidence stacked up against him. But now the situation was different. It was becoming more serious and complicated, and her father was under the spotlight now.

But she was not interested in who did it or what their motives were. All she knew was that she wanted her mother back. Nothing more than that. She felt a pain striking her head.

'You have organised all of this, you villain! You came to my house with the intention to ruin it. You'd better confess now," said Jalal, launching another attack on Ghassan.

Ghassan smiled coldly, adjusted himself in his seat, and leaned over towards Jalal.

"Is this a new game, Jalal? Do you want to deceive me again?" he whispered.

The room's attention shifted back to Jalal, who could not hide his awkwardness. Khalifa and Ali were shifting their eyes between the two men, trying to figure out this new piece of the puzzle, which was a mystery to them but clearly understood by Jalal. He lowered his head and rubbed his hands. Everyone was waiting for an answer. Events that had been closed off for decades might now have to be opened and examined and brought into the light.

Chapter 13

I was coming out of the mosque, after I had spent nearly an hour with Othman, the Sudanese sheikh, studying the sciences of the Holy Quran and its interpretation. The sheikh always stressed the importance of restoring the Ummah to its former glory, regretting its decline and complaining of the seditions and sins that abound in this time. He said the time must come to change all this, no matter how far people had transgressed nor how much corruption had increased. God's victory was inexorably coming.

As I was leaving the mosque, I heard someone calling

from inside. "Ghassan… Ghassan… Stop". It was Jalal.

"Jalal? What are you doing here? How could not I not have noticed your presence while you were there?"

"I have just entered the mosque to look for you, they mentioned that you had just left it a few seconds ago."

Your presence there had been a pleasant surprise to me, Jalal. I had always been trying to convince you to join the group and keep Quran's company, despite that you had always been busy, apologising, and procrastinating.

You talked while you were gasping, trying to pull yourself together. You handed me a sky-blue covered book and a piece of paper. In your hand you held another piece of paper, which contained a table of names that I did not recognise. I looked puzzled.

"When I entered the mosque, I saw a boy looking for you," you said. "He gave me this paper from Sheikh Othman, who had asked that it be handed to you. He requests that you write your name and put your signature next to it."

"I was with Sheikh Othman a little while ago, but he did not tell me anything about this. What is this register of names for?"

I started turning the paper, looking through it another time while I wondered what this could be about.

You shrugged your shoulders.

"The boy said it is a list of people who wish to join the group going to Mecca," you said. We are now in the seventh of Dhul Qa'dah (the month before pilgrimage season), and there is not much time left to travel."

I racked my brain, trying to connect the dots. I could remember conversations with Sheikh Othman about that subject and the eagerness I had expressed to participate in the Hajj pilgrimage this year. He apologised at the outset and had said it was too late, the registration deadline had passed. After I had pestered him, he promised to see if he could add my name to the list of pilgrims.

"What about these two books?"

"I have no idea. He said that they came from Kuwait and that it might interest you and that you will find out what it means."

I had leaned the paper on the wall then took out a pencil from my pocket, wrote my name hastily, signed next to it, and then handed it to you.

"Do not forget our date tonight at your father's farm," you said.

I hit my forehead with my arm.

"I am terribly sorry, Jalal, I cannot," I apologised. "I will be going to Mr Saleh's house tonight. Did you forget it is Tuesday, which is my weekly date to visit my fiancée? I cannot miss that."

"Oh, you traitor! Are you renouncing your old friends for a woman, whom you have known for less than two months?"

I laughed, blushing with embarrassment, and tried to salvage the situation.

"Do not change your plans. Tell the guys that the date has not changed and I will ask one of the workers to open the gates and set up a place for you. I will make this up to you soon, I promise."

You made a face that faked pain. You came close to me, put your arms around me, closed your eyes and said,

"On a date with happiness, we were... we were far away and on hope, we lived..."

I shook with laughter as you sang one of Talal's songs. I tried to move away from you while you buried your face in my chest, faking cries.

"Oh, dear lovers, how could the fire of fondness be extinguished," you went on.

"How could separation wipe out the memory of the eyes... the look of longing and the sweetest years... that we had lived, my grieving heart..."

"I do not think Talal would be pleased to hear such a bad imitation. He would bury himself alive from depression."

I had finally succeeded in moving you away. I slipped the paper in your jalabiya as you finished off your performance, wiping away imaginary tears and turning back to the mosque. I remembered something important, so I shouted at you from a distance as you were about to disappear behind the fence of the mosque.

"Do not mess with the palm trees. My father would kill me if anything bad happened to them, do you hear me?"

My voice echoed around the place unanswered.

I had a feeling this night would be tough for my father (like every visit to the farm from my friends). Then I heard your voice behind me as you peered over the top of the fence.

"Destinies!"

****

Later that night I knocked on Mr Saleh's door. A few seconds passed until the door opened to Lamyea all primped up.

I stayed at her house late that night. The time flew by while we exchanged love, affection and passion. She was shy in a way that made her more attractive, saying nothing except for a few words in the beginning but by the end we were both spilling secrets to each other. We started planning our future. I told her about my desire to pursue my studies abroad, and although I was concerned about her reaction to this, she nodded her head and said she did not care where she lived as long as she was with me.

That night I fell asleep with a smile that never left my lips. I recalled every whisper, giggle and joke. The image of her filled my mind. She had a wondrous ability to make me forget about the world and all that was going around me, making me feel like my true self. A week later, I woke up to grave news that changed not only my life, but would affect everyone around me.

****

Chapter 14

A mobile phone rang, disrupting the silence. Ghassan grabbed his phone and without a flicker crossing his face, excused himself and went into the other sitting room to take the call.

Jalal shook his knees nervously and whispered to Khalifa, while jerking his head towards his rival in the other room.

"He is manipulating us. I know him well. He will play these games one after the other."

Khalifa rubbed his bald head and sighed.

"We have no other choice," he told Jalal. "If that man was

the one who kidnapped your wife or had anything to do with it, then we ought to encourage him to speak. Perhaps we could catch a thread of truth by doing so. It seems that this truth might unleash far more than what we expect!"

Khalifa seemed perplexed. He and Jalal had met at the nearby mosque when he had moved into the area, and then again at various social occasions. The bonds of friendship between them and their families had flourished ever since. But the relationship had always been formal, despite how frequently they met.

He pointed at Khatir and whispered to Jalal,

"There is no doubt that what is happening is beyond the endurance of a boy of his age."

Jalal looked at his son, who was sitting absent-mindedly in a far corner, his eyes reddened. Sadness crept over Jalal. He was full of sorrow about what was happening to his family.

"He is the closest to her and she has always favoured him over the rest," Jalal told Khalifa. "She gives him her utmost care and attention. They sing the same songs and love the same food. If you went into his room, you would find him putting pictures of her in his closet. I have always felt jealous of him."

A muffled laugh came out from his mouth, contrasting with the tears in his eyes. Khalifa looked at him with pity and patted his neighbour on the shoulder.

"You have raised him well, Jalal. The masculinity of boys starts to be defined and formulated at this age. The first woman a man deals with in his life is his mother. You can tell a lot about someone and decide up to what level you can trust him just from the way he treats his mother."

Ghassan returned to where they sat. He apologised for his absence, saying that it was a call from his boss who was furious because he missed his plane and had ordered him to leave as soon as possible. Jalal's wrath returned.

"We do not have time for such tricks."

"We need to listen, Jalal."

Khalifa pointed at him. Ghassan began to mock.

"What is the matter, Jalal? Are you afraid of the truth?"

"Which truth? And what is this nonsense that you keep talking about? My wife has been missing for hours, I have no idea where she is, and here we sit to listen to this fool, all the while we are running out of time!"

"Calm down, Jalal. You have to calm down if you want to find your wife. Please!"

At that moment, Jalal got up and rushed towards the big cupboard that housed the television, opened one of its drawers, took out a small yellow hand-size bag, and opened its zipper, showing the contents to everyone in the room.

"We have wasted hours chatting and mumbling, while she is off the grid, with no supplies or medication. She is supposed to take them as soon as she wakes up. She cannot function without her medication nor the oxygen cylinder. She might experience shortness of breath at any moment and who is there to aid her? All this might be happening now while we are here having this little chat!"

No-one said a word, while Jalal gasped in agitation. He threw the medication bag on the table in the corner of the room. Everyone sensed the gravity of the situation. The only noise was the quiet crying of Khatir.

After a few moments, Ghassan spoke.

"The first to hit, yet also the first to cry and then file a complaint. You insist on playing the victim every time, but you never dare to admit your mistakes and your misbehaviour. Shouldn't you just confess so we can all be done with this?"

Jalal stood up, spewing out all sorts of insults and swearing at Ghassan. Ali stood up to try to restrain his furious father-in-law, and asked his wife to take her brother upstairs so he would not hear anything worse. Sara had grabbed Khatir and took him upstairs, before Khalifa managed to gain control and get everyone to sit down.

"We do not understand. What is the reason behind such talk?," he asked Ghassan. "What do you refer to when narrating these events that had happened many years ago? What happened after that?"

Ghassan inhaled deeply to restore himself to calm, picking up where he had left off.

"What had happened after that was a real catastrophe. It nearly made people lose their minds!"

****

Chapter 15

In the early hours of the first day of the Hijri year, during the tranquillity of the dawn and the serenity of the holy mosque in Mecca, multitudes of worshippers finished their prayer while surrounding the Kaaba in a sphere of spirituality that had spread throughout the Temple Mount.

All of the sudden, a group of nearly 300 armed men popped up, spreading through the Temple Mount of the sacred mosque. Shots were fired at the sky of Mecca and near the holy Kaaba. They called themselves "The Mohtasib Salafist Group", operating under the leadership of their head "Juhaiman".

A thick-bearded man rushed towards the solemn Imam, wielding a dagger at his face. He pulled the microphone away from the Imam and shouted instructions to his followers, who spread among the halls of the Mount. They quickly closed all the gates and mounted the high beacons, using them as convenient shooting positions to open fire on the crowds.

The man with the bushy beard started shouting via the speaker system, "Allah Akbar… Allah Akbar… Al Mahdi Al Mahdi". He fired several shots, to the terror of the tens of thousands of Muslims held captive inside. Fear and panic filled people's hearts as everyone tried to find an escape. Dead bodies fell on the ground of the sacred mosque while some innocents kept praying and pleading to God.

News spread quickly all over the world. The greatest tragedy was that the most sacred place, its rituals and the security of the religion itself, had been targeted. The Holy mosque had been occupied!

The incident was terrible beyond imagination. Some

thought that it had hidden dimensions and was the result of other, underlying factors. While others believed that it was the end of eternity, a doomsday event, as nothing could be more terrible than shedding blood on the grounds of the pure holy mosque, occupying it, damaging it, opening fire beside the Kaaba and killing many people.

The Temple Mount was totally emptied of worshippers. Bullets had penetrated the wall of the mosque and the columns of the beacons. The voice of one of the rebels echoed through the speakers, as he praised the characteristics of the Mahdi, his time, and those who joined him. They said everyone must pledge allegiance to him and obey him.

Outside, the Saudis had frantically mobilised their entire military forces. Hundreds of policemen and dozens of military personnel surrounded the site. Many statesmen and ministers arrived, but given the greatness and seriousness of the matter, the authorities did not dare to burst into the sanctity of the Holy Mosque until a written advisory was issued through the general Mufti of the Kingdom giving permission in this case.

The military commander spoke through a loudspeaker from outside the mosque and issued a warning to the terrorists inside.

"In the name of Allah, the Merciful, the Munificent, to whoever is inside the Temple Mount, the work you have done is not gratified by Allah. His Majesty King Khalid bin Abdul Aziz gives you this warning - give yourselves up, and lay down your weapons! You will be judged by Allah, the almighty and glorious…"

Silence prevailed for a few moments. Then the rebels answered the warning by opening fire on the policemen. Many on both sides fell. One of Johiman's followers began shouting to his comrades to attack and shoot at the military personnel, causing destruction and havoc in the holiest places.

The blockade of Mecca lasted for two full weeks; it was a terrible nightmare for everyone. On the fourth of December,

Saudi authorities managed to take control from the rebels, who had left hundreds of dead in the square of the holy mosque. Those left alive, including their leader, Johiman, were arrested. Sixty-three people were subsequently sentenced to death in eight different cities of the Kingdom of Saudi Arabia.

On the other side of the country, and in our humble and remote village, I was awaiting a destiny unknown that turned my life into a living hell.

****

Chapter 16

Everyone was listening to Ghassan as he continued to tell his story from 1979, including Sara, who had finally managed to stop Khatir's sobbing and shivering. He ended up falling into a deep sleep after growing tired of crying. She had patted his hair and kissed his forehead before she went down to rejoin the rest of the circle in the living room.

Jalal's cynical voice broke in.

"Have I not told you that he is playing us? Is this the right time to present such a historical lecture?"

"The fact that I am brighter, more knowledgeable, and

enlightened, has always provoked you since we were at school. It has always been infuriating to you when you see that I am more special. Do not blame me if your mental abilities do not serve you to reach my level!"

"Enough!," Khalifa yelled at them, putting an end to the repetitive bickering.

Everyone kept quiet, including the detective. He was perplexed by the state of the family. At the beginning he thought it was a family dispute, which the wife had taken advantage of to teach her husband a lesson he would never forget. The husband's panic was excessive and concerning. Things had evolved from being lost to being kidnapped to now potentially being killed. He had been certain that it was a trick from her, then suspicion turned to Ghassan, when all fingers pointed at him. And now here he was, finding yet another suspect. The situation had become extremely complicated.

Khalifa directed himself to Sara.

"I want you to bring me your mother's mobile phone," he

ordered. "We have to check it out immediately. Perhaps it will provide us with a more efficient methodology, or give us a clue about what has happened, saving us lots of these desperate arguments."

He glared at Ghassan and Jalal. Sara went upstairs towards her parents' bedroom to search for the phone. Khalifa sighed, took off his thick glasses and pressed a small handkerchief on his bulging eyes, squeezing at the tears that constantly covered them and then examined the wet napkin before him.

"Things cannot be solved by all this shouting and arguing. We have become immersed in the events and we have lost sense of where we are. Listen to me. When you face a problem, any problem, you have to step back and pause for a bit to look at the case as a whole in its entire surroundings, as if you were standing before a huge painting. If you stand very close, the colours blend together in front of your eyes and the details are all jumbled in your mind. You are not able to realise its beauty and see the true picture unless you step back to view it in its entirety . Some things look beautiful only when we step back from them. "

No-one gave a comment. He sounded reasonable, and he had succeeded in easing the tension between them. Jalal rested his head on his hand in sorrow.

"What are we going to do now?" Ali asked.

"Do you believe what that counterfeiter has said?"

Jalal raised his voice sharply while pointing at his enemy.

"You direct questions at me! He has totally succeeded in convincing you. He is lying. He is a liar and ignorant, revelling in everything he has said!"

Ghassan laughed sarcastically and rubbed his chin.

"Everything has become crystal clear now. The truth is as clear as day. There is no room for games and trickery. Your wife's life is in grave danger and you should reveal where she is. You must not let money blind your eyes from reality. "

Shouts and roars filled the room once again, much more intense this time. Ghassan's words had been like a red rag to a bull and Jalal rushed towards with all his might, grabbing him by the neck, shouting furiously.

"You are the reason all of this has happened! You are the curse that insists on befalling me no matter how far away you go. Calamities have not stopped raining down upon us since the moment you came through that door. I swear that I will break your neck with my bare hands."

Khalifa and Ali had rushed to separate the two men, just as Sara returned to the room from upstairs. She ran towards them, shouting at them to let go of each other.

"The tank... the oxygen tank of my mother..." she said, speaking quickly, struggling to get the words out. "It was there in her room when we arrived, but it has disappeared now!"

Everyone looked startled, needing a few seconds to absorb the information they had just received. Jalal pushed Ghassan back and rushed upstairs, before returning again a few minutes later. His face was a picture of great bafflement. He threw his body on the sofa, wailing.

"It is not there! Indeed, it was there, but it is no longer there now!"

"What does this mean? Is she here? Is she here with us?,"Sara asked, bewildered, her jaw shaking as she tried to hold back tears. Everyone looked at each other, searching for an answer to the conundrum. Khalifa turned to Ghassan.

"What had happened after the catastrophe at Mecca?," he asked, confounding everyone with the change of subject.

Ghassan took off his gold-rimmed glasses to reveal glassy and shiny eyes. He gave Jalal a look of admonishment, before taking a deep breath.

****

Chapter 17

We were following the updates of the case closely, as there was a shortage of information about what had gone on. I was sitting next to my father at our house, reading the newspaper and on the front of the first page in bold type it said -

"A Rebel Armed Group Infiltrates the Sacred Mosque Calling Out that One of them is The Awaited Mahdi!"

"The competent authorities have taken all measures to control the situation!"

"According to The Opinion of All Scholars, Measures

Have Been Taken to Protect Muslims' Lives!"

"Strong International Islámic Condemnation of The Terrorist Act!"

"Twelve Million Riyals donated by His Majesty King Khalid to The Martyrs of The Temple Mount!"

Headlines were blazoned across the pages, with information that included a description of the incident, the numbers involved, names of all the rebels who were caught and executed and names of other people involved that had multiple nationalities. Then my eyes caught sight of something that pierced my heart and made my throat turn dry.

"Name: Othman Jamal Sidiq- Nationality; Sudanese"

I felt dizzy and the ground seemed to spin under my feet. I reread the names until I reached the name of Sheikh Othman again, who was included among more than 60 names of different nationalities and origins. The shock had tied my tongue and paralyzed my brain, nothing could get me out of it, until there was a heavy knock on the door. My legs shook as I went to open it, finding policemen standing before me. Once they confirmed my identity, they threw me in the back of their car and set out to where I did not know.

I had been imprisoned on charges of belonging to the Salafist group. They had found my name on a list of those who had joined the rebellion to occupy the holy mosque, as well as my signature pledging allegiance to Mahdi. They had also found books of "Juhaiman and his followers" in my room, which had been imported from Kuwait.

My father spent three days tirelessly going to the police station, pleading, crying for the loss of his son, unsure if he would ever see me again.

I was finally released from prison after clarifying everything and signing pledges, and my innocence was proven. However, the people of the village never released me from their prison of suspicion and doubt. News of my alleged belonging to the group spread far and wide. "Ghassan, the son of the wealthy dates trader, was detained on charges of rebellion and treason," they repeated to each other. No matter how innocent I actually was, I could not shake the scandal. I became tainted, people's perception of me had differed, and their eyes shot arrows of accusation at me without anyone saying a single word.

Things did not stop there - in fact they got much worse. The night following my release, Lameya's father came to our farm in a rage, asking to break up the engagement. He stopped on the doorstep, refusing to cross the threshold, as if even entering this disgraced house would cause a stigma.

Mr Saleh shouted at me and my father while he pointed his hands at us. He announced that he would not allow his daughter to marry a man with a tarnished security record and had been accused of belonging to a terrorist group.

I held his hands, pleading with him.

"Please, uncle. The whole thing was built on falsehood. Everything will become clear soon, for sure."

My father stepped in.

"Mr Saleh, you are a wise and reasonable man. You cannot believe such things."

Lameya's father pulled his hand away from mine in disgust. He looked at me and my stunned father.

"Because I am a wise man, who has a brain, I cannot accept your traitor son as a husband for my wife anymore," he said, stressing every word. "I have always wished God's blessings for my daughter, but there is no goodness in such affinity!"

He looked at us askance for a few seconds before he turned around. I asked if I could see her and talk to her. But he said he would choose a husband for his daughter by himself and that he would not trust money, family name, nor prestige as he has done before; since my high financial status had not matched up with my low moral level, as he believed them to be.

My world had been turned upside down, all the colours and pleasures of life vanished from my eyes. Life became hollow of happiness in those moments. How could the same thing be your source of pleasure and agony at the same time? I had lost everything, through no fault of my own. Do you know why? It was your selfishness, Jalal!

"You set me up. You brought me the names list yourself, and you made up the story of the pilgrimage out of pure malice. You faked the whole story about a boy handing the piece of paper to you to give to me. You gave me that suspicious book that led to the charges against me. I know now that boy did not exist. It was all your deception and deep-rooted malevolence.

It saddens me that I could only find out the truth after I left Al-Ahsaa with no return. When I was accepted to study abroad, I did not hesitate for a second. Yes… I ran away from everything; it is hard to live your life as someone falsely accused. I escaped from everything that could remind me of that village and what had happened there. Yet memories are like a burning sun, they shine right above your head, to keep forcing you to see the hidden shadows of your reflection.

CHAPTER 17

Only two months had passed since my departure when I received the news of your marriage from Lameya. My father had long avoided answering my constant questions about her until he revealed the news, which left me distraught and feeling much resentment towards both of you. I felt like I had been terribly betrayed. I hated everything that brought us together, our friendship, our childhood. The memories only worsened the treachery against me.

I spent my life immersed in work, all day until the night fell with its harshness and miseries. I used to lie in my bed staring at the ceiling of my bedroom, and every day, two thin lines of tears dropped from the sides of my eyes until sleep gave me respite from my grief. Then I would wake up the next morning to another bleak day.

****

Chapter 18

"You are lying... you are lying!"

Everyone's features had frozen as Ghassan's words fell on them like a destructive thunderbolt. Jalal's cries as he denied the accusations from Ghassan were harrowing.

The situation had just become more complicated and more confusing. This was the most difficult moment the family had ever faced, when they had to decide what and who to believe amidst the volleys of accusations, which had made them witnesses to a brutal battle between facts and doubts. It was hard to believe someone they thought of as an angel for all these years could have been a demon, it was beyond the brain's capacity to swallow.

Everyone in the room was lost for words including Khalifa, who did not know what to say. It seemed that a new picture was starting to become apparent. Jalal kept screaming.

"He is lying... You do not understand!"

Ghassan stopped him, victory clearly in his eyes.

"I moved away to avoid us ever meeting and having to reveal the truth. But you insisted on it and in front of all of your family members, too. You have left me no choice. Where did I lie, exactly? Tell me, did you not give me that list?"

"Yes, but it..."

"Did not you hand me those books?"

"Yes, I did hand them to you..."

"Did you not marry my fiancé, only two months after our breakup?"

"Yes, but it does not seem..."

"Everyone..."

Ghassan interrupted Jalal again, and turned to the rest of the audience.

"It is very clear that this man hatched a despicable plot against me, and then married Lameya to control her wealth. He wanted to get rid of me, so he had me implicated in a dangerous security issue. When I threatened him yesterday, she felt vulnerable and he was afraid that all he had planned would vanish with the wind. Now he is getting rid of Lameya to possess all her wealth. What malice!"

Disappointment and disgust directed towards Jalal swept through the room, the harshest looks of all was from his daughter, who was standing beside the door with tearful eyes and wet cheeks after all that she had heard. There were too many shocks for her to endure. The lofty edifice of her father was collapsing before her eyes and crumbling to dust.

"Wait!" It was Ali.

He got up from his seat and headed slowly towards the corner of the sitting room. He scanned it with his eyes, and turned to the cupboard housing the television, opening its drawers under the questioning glares of the others. He turned while he was looking at the side of the cupboard.

"The bag of medicine that was there on that table - where is it now?"

Everyone turned around in search of it, except for Jalal, who was distressed.

"What makes this important now? It is either on the table or in the cupboard, it will not change a thing…"

"But it would change a lot, uncle. I suspect something. I do not want to get carried away, though. I do not wish to hear someone saying that my psychology specialism has affected my brain. "

Khalifa could sense his hesitation. He stood near him and patted his shoulder to encourage him.

"Say what you are thinking. We will not lose any more time than we have already lost."

Ali's eyes looked at his wife, whose eyes were swollen with redness. She had lost her strength, so she sat on the nearest chair she could find. He also looked at her father. Ali took a few moments, as he was reluctant to reveal his thoughts. Then he made up his mind to speak.

"Who was sitting there when my uncle threw the medicine bag on this table in the corner of the hall?"

No-one gave an answer, since none knew the purpose of such an inquiry. Khalifa caught the meaning swiftly, however, and in return, directed his own question to the room.

"When we lost the oxygen tank, who was the only absentee from the scene at that moment?"

Sara gasped, and put her hand over her mouth. Jalal's eyes widened in surprise.

"Are you kidding me? We are in the middle of a very serious situation!"

"Please, uncle, give me a chance. Sit and I will explain everything from my point of view."

But Jalal shouted in the face of his son-in-law.

"Are you going to give us a lecture here... and now? I have always perceived you as the most reasonable!"

"Typical Jalal," Ghassan piped up from the corner. "Excuse him… he is afraid in front of anyone more knowledgeable and prestigious than him!"

Jalal glared at him, full of resentment.

Ali started to speak.

"One mental complication that becomes a psychological complex in humans develops during their early years. It is connected to their parents. When the child is between five and eight years of age, he gets attached to one of his parents, which is totally normal and rather healthy, in fact. But in some cases that attachment might develop too far, until it turns to a different kind of love and affection. In addition, they can hate to share their beloved. So, he feels jealous of his father unconsciously and without him realising it, sees him as a barrier between himself and his mother. In many cases, he sees his mother favouring his father over him and giving him an advantage in some behaviours over others."

Everyone was listening. Ali knew each word he spoke was of grave importance.

"However, possessing his mother can often elude him, of course. So the child imitates his father, and tries to be a smaller version of him, hoping to get the same attention and special treatment. Freud, the Austrian doctor, introduced this personality complex, which he called the "Oedipus complex" or the "Paternity complex", which the son might experience in his younger years. But it seems that what we have here in front of us is a rare condition…"

"This is nonsense!" shouted Jalal. "Are you going to accuse my son of some sort of sickness or madness merely for his attachment to his mother, like all children have?"

"You know that it is not a mere attachment, uncle!" Ali said. "Have you not noticed that Khatir is always trying to mimic your way of speaking, dressing, and behaving? Do you know how old your son is now? He is more than 12. Have you not noticed how many times he has wanted to sleep in your bed? Have you not noticed his weird behaviour, which has long embarrassed his mother. Like when he was touching her body in front of us? Can you not remember how you have always felt jealous of him?"

Silence prevailed on everyone, including Jalal, who did not know what to say. Ali continued.

"This does not mean that all children suffer from the complex in the same way. Some might come across it and get over it without anyone really noticing, some never experience it at all. While some might go through it because of the misbehaviour of the parents, which might worsen the case!"

Jalal shook his head, refusing to believe what Ali was saying.

"But this is crazy! A child of that age cannot do such a thing."

"But it seems very logical,"Khalifa intervened, sounding professional and objective. "Look at things from his point of view - that he deserves her more than you - and then think back over what happened yesterday. It was beyond his endurance, to see his rival slapping his mother right before his eyes. He decided that you do not deserve her."

Khalifa turned and pointed at Ghassan, who was following the developments closely. Then he took the piece of paper with the threatening note from his pocket.

"The presence of this man came at the right time, so it seems. He was the source of the conflict that Khatir witnessed, so he used the words he heard from Ghassan's mouth and wrote them on this paper.

Ghassan lowered his head in embarrassment at hearing the empty threats once again.

"And because using his handwriting to deliver the message would reveal his identity, he typed it using his computer and printed it so the font would be neutral and less suspicious."

No-one spoke. The theory sounded entirely plausible. The twists and turns were making everyone feel dizzy, but despite how unpalatable it was, the incident now made sense. Jalal could not take any more, so he threw his body on the sofa. Ali sat beside him.

"He has not done this to hurt anybody, he loves her to

the extent of adoration," he said, sympathetically . "This is scientifically proven."

Jalal did not give an answer, he was lost for words. He was looking at the empty space in front of him with bleary eyes. His body slumped, a contrast to the simmering rage and agitation of a few minutes ago. His silence felt heavy on everyone.

Ghassan felt sad at how the events were turning out, lowering his head towards the floor. Ali and Khalifa exchanged a knowing look, then Khalifa sighed in sorrow and stood up.

"And now… Where is Khatir?"

"I am here!"

The voice was shaky, coming from upstairs. Everyone's necks craned round to see him coming down the stairs taking wobbly and terrified steps, his eyes full of tears and terror.

****

Chapter 19

Jalal snapped out of his stupor and with wide and scary eyes, he pounced at Khatir, who had barely stepped into the sitting room. His father pulled him violently and slapped his face until he dropped to the floor. Then he pulled him up by his shirt, shouting into his face.

"You bastard. Tell me, where is your mother now? Come on, where is she?"

He gave him a second slap, but this brought about no response other than more crying and weeping and the boy put his hands to his face to shield himself from the blows. The rest of the men rushed at Jalal, fearing that his wrath would result in a new catastrophe, and pushed him to the other side of the hallway. Sara ran to her brother, who was barely able to stand. She sat beside him and hugged his head tenderly. Jalal kept screaming.

"I swear, I will kill you with my bare hands, you stupid child. Tell me where your mother is immediately!"

"Why do you care about her now?"

Jalal's shouts faded after hearing his son speak. His voice sounded different - it seemed stern, and his sharp glares shocked him.

"You do not deserve her," said Khatir. "She will always be better off without you. You have always been a source of disturbance and distress to her, while I have not. And in return, she favours you every time over me. You do not deserve her. You do not deserve her!"

A thick vein stood out on the boy's forehead as he screamed.

"You foolish, sick boy," Jalal screamed back. "I will suffocate you to death if you do not tell me where she is now!"

Khatir's cries increased and he buried his face in his sister's lap. His father was breathless but knew strength and shouting were no longer useful with his broken son. He lowered his head and then spoke to him in a tender and quiet voice.

"We have always loved you so much, my son. She favours you in many things. Do you remember how she always keeps the chicken dish for you and won't let anyone else start eating it before you? Do you remember how she always buys the most recent games for you? Can you remember that time when we went to the public park and then you got lost all of a sudden? She was about to lose her mind. She rushed around crying and searched all around the park, asking everyone she came across if they had seen you. She loves you, my son… She loves you very much."

A hot tear dropped from Jalal's eyes, a contrast to the stiffness of his features. He looked to see if his words had any influence on Khatir. The boy waited for a few moments before speaking, his voice heavy with tears.

"I didn't mean to cause problems, I swear I did not mean to hurt her. I wanted to protect her from everything and from you, but I did not imagine it would turn to this. I wanted to teach you a lesson that you would never forget, I wanted you to understand that she is the most important of all things, to understand that there is one who loves her more than you."

Jalal and Ghassan exchanged looks. Khatir wiped the tears from his chin.

"But everything got out of control," he said, "and I was so scared when I heard you talking about her sickness and how severe it is. Then I realised the full extent of the catastrophe, which I have brought on everyone. I wanted to fix that mistake, so I took her medication and the oxygen tank."

"Please, son," Jalal interrupted. "We all need her. She will get hurt if we do not rescue her now. Please just tell me where she is."

Jalal gave him a sympathetic look, but Khatir's expression hardened. He became sterner and harsher.

"But everything is because of you. I deserve her more than you, you do not deserve her, and you will not get her ever! She is in a better place than she was. She is enjoying her time more than she used to when she was with you."

Jalal felt his patience for this useless children's game running out. He had to find her in his own way and as quickly as he could, he rushed at Khatir. Sara stepped in to protect Khatir and shouted in her father's face.

"I know where she is! I know where my mother is!"

Sara asked her father and husband to follow her quickly. The three hurried across the hall of the house, then they entered the kitchen, where its outer door led to the backyard.

"She must be there."

She pointed at the backyard that was empty except for an old wooden cupboard and an old water tank. Suddenly everything became clear to Jalal and he rushed towards it. Khatir, his mother, and the tank - everything now made sense in his head. While he was trying to open the small, locked door, he stuck his face in close and started shouting.

"Lameya! Are you here? Can you hear me?"

He fixed his ear on the surface of the tank, trying to catch the sound of any movement that would prove his daughter's guess was correct. Sara stood next to her husband, anxiously biting her nails at the kitchen door. Ali rushed to get a hammer from inside and then hit the lock twice until it cracked and fell on the ground.

Jalal pushed his son-in-law aside and opened the tank door to a whoosh of heavy and wet air. Inside, he saw her body lying on the wet, dark ground, her skin and nightgown were drenched in sweat.

Jalal crawled inside and found the oxygen tank near her. He put the mask on her nose and turned on the wheel to release the gas. He hugged her head and started to stroke her hair gently, calling her name.

"Lameya... Lameya, please wake up. Everything will be fine, just open your eyes, please! I promise you will never be hurt again. We all need you here, my dear. Wake up, my love, wake up."

He put his head on her forehead and started crying. He had lost her forever, his wife and companion on his journey through life. He cried for himself and he cried for her. He sobbed at how things had ended up - only yesterday he had a happy and strong family, and now he had lost everything in a blink of an eye. He had lost his wife at the hands of his son! How could his life continue now?

Ali hugged his pregnant wife, they cried over their loss beside the big empty water tank, where the old man sat, hugging his wife's head sorrowfully.

But then, from inside that white cavity and under that oxygen mask, there was a small cough.

****

Chapter 20

The big house was noisy. Many footsteps were going here and there while much humming was emanating from the room. There were many rectangular boxes scattered on the floor and people were forming a circle around the wide bed.

It was a bit painful when Lameya opened her eyes. Everything around her was hazy and foggy, her head was wrapped by a bandage and an oxygen mask was placed on her mouth.

The first person she noticed was the one sitting next to her, stroking her hair and looking at her with a mixture of happiness and anxiety. In fact, Jalal had not left her side until the ambulance had arrived. Even then he held her hands as the paramedics delivered her aid, running alongside the stretcher as they carried her inside, shouting at them to hold her gently.

"Jalal.." A faint call came from her mouth. Her husband leant in and whispered while he stroked her hands

"I am here, darling, don't worry everything will be okay. We are all here for you. Look who's here…"

Sarah ran to her mother's bedside and started kissing her face and hands as she cried. Lameya cried at her daughter's tears and tried to reassure her as her own tears flowed through the words. Meanwhile, Ali was standing next to the door of her bedroom.

"Thank God for your safety,aunt. We were very worried about you. We really care about you and pray that you regain full health and wellness," he said.

Lameya was about to respond to her daughter's husband, but she suddenly noticed a shade behind him. It was Khatir, looking worriedly from a distance at his mother. As soon as she saw him, she felt a lump in her throat. She raised her hands toward him and signalled him to come.

He hesitated and he looked at his father while tears filled his eyes. Jalal gazed at him for a while, then he took a deep breath and gestured to him to come inside. Khatir ran into his mother's arms and started sobbing. He hid his face in her chest and asked her to forgive him.

"Everything is okay, darling. Don't worry, I'm okay," Lameya said.

"It's time to leave the room now so the rest of the medical team can provide treatment for your mother," the paramedic said, interrupting the intimate family reunion. "She desperately needs rest and calmness, away from any kind of agitation."

Jalal went downstairs and found Khalifa talking on his phone about his work, while Ghassan stayed quiet and played with his mobile. Jalal felt guilty. He thought that everything would have been peaceful after meeting his old friend after many years of absence. When they met each other by coincidence he thought that their old days would have come back to them. But things turned out to be more damaged and messier than he thought, and the gap between the two former friends had widened.

Once Khalifa finished his call, Jalal spoke to him, stuttering and rubbing his hands together in shame.

"I am... I'm really sorry about everything that has happened in my house. I apologise for bothering you with our problem and I appreciate all your efforts and patience. Without... Without you, we would not have been able to solve this difficult that my family has come across. I owe you a lot."

Khalifa smiled sympathetically, relieved that everything was over. Ghassan had remained silent, then stood up.

"I do not think there is any point in me being here anymore. I will leave now."

Jalal got up and raised his hand.

"Please Ghassan," he begged. "Give me a chance to explain."

"There is nothing to explain, Jalal. I have been more offended in this house than I have ever been anywhere in my whole life."

He headed to the door, and as he was about to leave, he heard his old friend's voice behind him, as if he was about to throw his last spear at his back. "I met with your father before he died, you know."

Ghassan suddenly stopped, while his hand remained on the door handle. They were both silent until he turned to Jalal.

"What are you talking about?" he asked.

Jalal moved his gaze from Ghassan to Khalifa who was watching them with curiosity. He rubbed his hands.

"You have no idea about what happened," Jalal said. "Many things happened after you left. You have chosen to understand the situation from your own perspective without looking at reality."

Ghassan's brow furrowed. He returned to the room

wanting to understand what Jalal meant, his brain filled with confusion.

"What is this reality you are talking about? And how is my father related to all that happened?"

Jalal's voice cracked under Khalifa and Ghassan's questioning gaze. He stared at the space beside him while his mind travelled back in time to more than 30 years ago.

Chapter 21

What had happened shocked everyone, not only the village people and Lameya's father, but also me more than anyone else. At first, I thought there had to be a mistake or a misunderstanding behind the situation, because it was unthinkable that you had associated yourself with those kinds of groups.

I have always categorically rejected them, but when I discovered Shaikh Othman's name among the list of names who were facing the death sentence, it made things worse. Even though you were released after being interrogated, it was complicated, because you were a close friend of his for a long period of time.

I did not know what I should do. You were entangled and surrounded by many suspicions. Should I have avoided meeting you and been affected by the accusations against you? Or should I have confronted all the people's looks of disapproval and continued our friendship? You were just a body without a soul or joy at that time, and would not meet me.

I even used to sit outside the mosque and wait for you after finishing the prayers, but most of the time you did not pray in the mosque. And if you saw me by chance in the mosque, you would rush home. You did not give me a chance to help you and get you out of your current state.

I was even more surprised when I accidentally found out that you travelled abroad. You did not care about your old friend - you did not care to inform me that you were leaving. You even did not give me an opportunity to say goodbye, you ignored all our years together as if I did not even exist. I always went to your home to see if you had returned, or to wait for a letter from you. But none arrived.

Three weeks after your departure, I came out of the mosque after I finished the noon prayers on a hot day. When I was looking for my shoes, I heard a deep voice from behind me.

"How are you, Jalal?"

It was Mr Saleh putting his hand on my shoulder.

He was not in as good a state as before. He had become taciturn, he had got shabby looking and he no longer participated in the village meetings, having previously been the master of every one. The reason was his daughter's health condition, which had deteriorated rapidly after what had happened. He was devastated to see her suffering, and eventually took her to the King Faisal hospital in Al Hufuf so that she could receive better care and treatment.

Her condition stabilised and she returned to the village. Life began to smile on him again and he wanted to bring himself out of that miserable state in any possible way. He made a big dinner party and slaughtered many sheep to celebrate the return of his daughter's good health, inviting many from the village to join his feast. When I met him that day, he was looking very comfortable and in good spirits. We walked together along the road that led us to the middle of the village.

"Are you still in contact with your friend?", he asked, while looking down as we walked. . I did not know how I should answer him. I thought that he would never ask about you after what you had done. He noticed that the question had me flummoxed so he tried to reassure me.

"I just wanted to make sure that you are well. I have known you since you were a student at my school. I also know your father, he is a very good and generous man."

"The same as Ghassan and his family," I said, the words causing a lump in my throat.

Then I noticed his smile, which barely contained its disregard for my attempted defence of my old friend.

"Yes, he was. And because I used to see him as you think,

I was deceived. And it almost took my daughter's life and made me lose her forever."

The sadness appeared on his face as he remembered that sorrowful time. Then he looked at the sky, his eyes almost closed as he squinted in the sunlight and took a deep breath.

"Because of that, and to avoid this kind of deception again, I want to decide my daughter's destiny. I don't want to wait for her fate and for her to encounter the unknown."

"What do you mean?," I asked.

He stopped walking, turned to me and looked me in the eye.

"I want you to marry Lameya!"

I was tongue-tied. It was the last thing I expected. Thoughts were swirling in my mind and all my words disappeared.

"I consider you as my son, I have taught you and raised you since you were a child," he said, seeing my confusion. "And you do not belong to a certain party or group, you do not care about reforms and issues of change. You do not even pray regularly at the mosque."

I was embarrassed by the last part, but despite all of what he said, he had asked me to marry my friend's ex-fiancée. My throat dried up for a moment before I answered him, trying to sound neutral.

"I cannot do this. You were one of my best teachers and I was honoured to be your student - I used to wait for your class eagerly. But your request is out of the question. I cannot do this to my friend."

He stepped close to me and put his hand on my shoulder, a broken smile on his face.

"This is a noble stand on your part, Jalal, but I am a man that almost lost their daughter forever. Can you imagine that? She was in her best health over the past couple of months and she was a very active girl. But then she relapsed, and it could have taken her life."

The signs of sadness appeared in his watery eyes. I remained silent, his request was just too difficult to weigh up. On one side was my old friend and on the other side, there was

Lameya, the girl that I loved until fate chose another man for her. When I saw her for the first time, I could not sleep that night and her face is still imprinted on my memory.

Mr Saleh interrupted my thoughts.

"Your friend has gone on his way to continue his life. Maybe he would be sad for a day or so, but he will return with a new happy life and after a couple of months, he will no longer think of what had happened. He had his opportunity, and now you and my daughter have a new chance to live together happily, and I am sure that you will be able to secure that for her."

I listened to him but I could not speak a word, and I knew he knew how shocked I was. He said that I must think carefully about his offer. Then he patted my shoulder and walked on his way, while leaving me alone to ponder his offer.

I was puzzled and could not decide what to do. I wished you were there, Ghassan, to give me your opinion or give me a nod of approval or not. I wanted any sign from you that would calm my anxiety and the feelings of guilt that washed over me. Then I decided to visit what you left behind, hoping to find an answer.

The next day, I was near the wall of your large farm just before sunset. We used to go up there together, but now it was empty except for me and your father, who was watering the tall palm trees quietly alone. He had taken to doing this after you left, as your departure had caused him so much sadness.

He was wrapping a tattered red shemagh around his head. He noticed me, but he continued his work silently. I also remained silent while I thought about what to say. While I was sitting on the tip of the water fountain, I could hear the sound of birds returning to their nests. Your father began to speak in his calm and quiet voice.

"Do you know why I took date palm trees as a trade?"

Some questions do not need an answer, and that was one of them. He went over to a palm tree and put his hand on the trunk.

"Although the palm tree is strong and solid, it has a soul the same as a human. Once the pith of a palm becomes weak or spoiled, then the whole tree will die."

He raised his head and looked at the high leaves of the tree.

"It's one of the most generous and precious creatures," he said, with a gaze as passionate as if looking upon a pretty woman. "It gives us all its parts. We use its trunk as pillars for our homes, and its leaves to shade us from the sun. We use its fibre to make rope and we eat its tasty fruit. It does not need much water, and will die if you water it too much. Do you know that the palm tree is mentioned in all the heavenly books?'

I felt the moment slipping, and I began to lose sight of the purpose of going there. I was about to speak but he continued.

"Do you know what is the most important part of the date palm tree and the part that is least valued by humans? This...'

He picked a curved and crusty branch from the ground that looked very old. "This is the most important part of the tree when we harvest the dates. It is called the cluster and without it, we would not be able to eat a single date. The cluster holds the heavy fruits while it is still connected to the tree trunk. It holds the heavy fruits for days and weeks, until it bends down towards the ground under the weight. However, it cannot separate from the trunk - if it does, then it dies, and all that it has been holding onto will also die. So it will not give up the fruits that it holds. We are ungrateful to it, and dismiss it. And this is how clusters end up.

So what if you were an old cluster? Go, dear, go and do what your heart is telling you to do."

He moved around, watering the palm tree whose bent leaves were giving him shade from the sunlight. I stayed where I was and looked at the palms in a different way than I used to do.

PART THREE
THE PALM PITH

This palm tree is the queen of the orchards

The princess of fields and the groom of the meadow.

It is the food of the poor and the dessert of the rich,

The chattel of the passenger and the stranger.

I feel astonished you are forgotten

and not celebrated by Arab poets and lyricists.

(Ahmad Shawki)

Chapter 23

MATERFI VILLAGE

1979

The day is done, and the night has wrapped the village in its dark curtain. People started to go back to their homes and let the darkness enjoy its time, amid the quiet and still. The narrow streets were deserted. However, on the far side of the village, three boys were sitting around a fire, the flames of which were reflected on their frightened faces.

Memories of that terrible accident at the spring still haunted them, filling their hearts with horror that lived inside their trembling hearts. What happened had shaken their entire world like a tremendous earthquake.

The accident demolished the arrogance and the violence they had carried inside them. The death of the leader of their group was a hideous unrelenting nightmare that insisted on visiting them every time they tried to sleep. The sight of his body being removed from the water was a vision none of them could ever forget.

They heard some hasty footsteps coming towards them. Between the branches of the palm trees, a messenger of one of the notable people of the village appeared. His arrival at that time, in that remote area, was an alarming sign that this was an urgent matter that could not be postponed. When the man reached the fire, only his stern eyes shone, the rest of his face was wrapped with a mask. He gestured to the youngest lad.

"My father wants to see you immediately," he whispered.

The boy was startled. If the issue involved Sheikh Salem, it did not bode well. His social status granted him leadership and guaranteed the full obedience of all villagers. In addition, his trade activities in the area - buying and selling land - boosted his status and authority. The only thing that would give him complete superiority in the village was leading prayers and ensuring adherence to the religious authorities. Then, he would control everything in the village, and nothing could be initiated or resolved unless he approved it.

The boy beside him trembled at the name of the Sheikh.

"What does he want with you?"

"It seems that his day is up, and we will follow him, no doubt of that!," lamented the third of their group.

"Do you have any idea about why the sheikh needs me?," asked the boy who had been called upon, his voice shaking.

"Get on your feet now, you will know everything when you meet him."

The boy looked to his comrades as if he was saying a final farewell, then went off with the man, who led him through the village roads towards the big house of Sheikh Salem. He was shown inside, to a dimly lit room filled with the smell of incense. Sheikh Salem was sitting in the middle of the room as he usually did. There was no one else there, apart from a man who followed him all the time and did not part from his side.

Sheikh Salem greeted the boy with a rigid face, devoid of any kindliness, which only stoked the boy's fears. He stroked his thick beard slowly while focusing his eagle eyes on the boy's lean body.

"Don't think for a moment that I'm ignorant of what you and your other reckless and irresponsible comrades did. I warned you before, but you insisted on committing mistakes because of your stubbornness and ignorance. Do I need to tell you about the fate of those who dare to violate Sheikh Salem's orders?"

He signalled to the guards outside the gate, the boy's bones shook in fear and his jaw started to tremble, words stuck inside his mouth. He stared at the space in front of him.

"Especially when this violation affects my family and my sons. I swear I will take revenge for my great loss and will never let it slide without punishment. I tasted bitterness and had to swallow it, but I will make you taste what is more bitter."

He got up from his seat and went closer to the boy until his huge, threatening body loomed over him.

"But I will forgive you, you are just like my son, he was as old as you and my heart will not allow me to hurt you or be cruel to you in any way. However, I demand the best from you in the future and you have to execute all that I ask you to do. Do you think you can do that, or should I change my mind and use torture on you?"

A drop of cold sweat slid down the face of the poor boy while he nodded his head, confirming his approval. His fear was beyond words, and he was ready to agree to whatever Sheikh Salem asked, just to get out of the place.

Sheikh Salem bent his body back and took another look at him. "What's wrong with your eyes?," he demanded.

The boy lowered his head in awkwardness.

"Someone threw sand from Om Zanbour Spring into my eyes, and since then they are protruding and always teary."

Sheikh Salem patted the boy's head tenderly and spoke in a wise and kind voice.

"You are a good boy, Khalifa."

***

In the afternoon of the following day, Khalifa walked to Al-Shaqiq village according to the instructions he had been given by the angry and grieving sheikh. Since losing his younger son, he had been eaten up by anger and hatred, which was targeted on those who caused the accident. He pretended to be calm and patient during the funeral ceremonies, but he was overwhelmed with grief and loss.

Sneaking into the village was a risky mission because of the conflict and hostility between the two villages. He got inside the lonely mosque and started looking for his target. He had been repeating the name the sheikh had given to him all the way to the mosque.

"Have you seen Ghassan Al-Kaheil?," he asked a young

man, only a little older than him, with curly hair. He was standing beside him in the middle of the mosque and when he turned to him, Khalifa stared at him for a few seconds because his vision was a bit hazy since the incident with the sand. His body trembled violently when he recognized the young man from that day at the springs.

He wanted to withdraw and give up the mission at once, but the threats of Sheikh Salem scared him more, so he made up his mind to complete the mission as soon as possible, before the young man in front of him could recognise him. He moved closer to him while looking to the side.

"Do you know Ghassan?"

"Yes, he is my friend. My name is Jalal, what's up?"

He answered spontaneously with a friendly smile on his face and that made Khalifa more perplexed. He stretched a trembling hand towards Jalal.

"These are for him, they are from the sheikh about the pilgrimage trips this year and these books are from Kuwait.

He will know about them once he sees them. Can you please ask him to write his name and sign this list and bring it back to me immediately. I'm in a hurry."

As soon as Khalifa handed over the paper and the books, he turned his back to conceal his face and hid in one of the corners of the mosque. He saw the young man with curly hair going outside the mosque.

A few minutes passed and Khalifa was sitting restlessly, consumed with fear and anxiety. He dearly wished he had not accepted this task and could just face his destiny with the sheikh, whatever that might be. It seemed to take forever for the young man to return. Finally, Jalal crossed the door holding the list in his hand and gave it to him with a beaming smile. Khalifa snatched the list quickly and hurried outside, breathing in relief. At that moment, Jalal shouted to him to stop.

He saw his fate flash vividly in front of his eyes - the young man must have recognised him, and the mission had failed. An intruder from Materfi village had sneaked into their village and been caught. This was enough for them to hang him to death at the entrance of the village. He froze where he stood but did not dare turn his back. His heart raced as Jalal came closer to him.

"Don't I deserve a word of thanks, at least?," asked Jalal.

Khalifa sighed in relief and kept his eyes on the exit.

"Thank you, generous young man."

He took a few slow steps out of the mosque, then accelerated and broke into a run. He hurried towards his village holding the paper tight, while a smile of happiness and relief crept over his face.

He ran away from Al-Shaqiq village, with everyone unaware of the consequences of the mission that he had just executed against people he did not know for reasons he did not know. However, that brief visit would have an impact on the lives of many people, the effects of which would still be felt 33 years later.

***

THE FINAL PART
THE FRUITS

More delicious than natural honey and

sweeter than the dessert of heavens

Fresher than embracing the beloved one after the breakup.

Chapter 24

AL-AHSA/AL-HAFOF

THURSDAY 17 MARCH 2016

T he clock on the wall of the house was pointing at 8:30 pm and everything was as it should be.

The lights outside the house were glittering, creating festive vibes. The family was having their best time ever. Everyone was gathered in the sitting room on the ground floor, balloons were scattered all around, and decorations and colourful ribbons were dangling from the ceiling. In the middle of the room, there was a rectangular table on which different types of drinks and desserts were carefully placed. And in the middle of the table, there was a large, rectangular cake.

Sara rushed towards her two-year-old child who was messing with the table. She carried him aside, and then adjusted her shiny black hair. Next to her, Ali was focusing the camera of his mobile on his son, Basim, who was standing next to the wall as he had been told to do in order to capture the best shot. Basim was putting a pen in his upper pocket and was wearing a headdress like his father. His appearance was causing much hilarity.

At that moment, Jalal came down the stairs to the ground floor holding Lameya's hand tenderly, she looked more beautiful and glowing than ever. She was wearing a maroon veil and her face was beaming with an innocent smile, the small mole crowning her upper lip, as it always had done. She looked at the preparations for the party with happiness and gratitude.

Jalal looked at her with love. He smiled when he saw her shining smile and focused his eyes on the details of her features with tenderness. Everyone rushed to congratulate them on their 35th wedding anniversary. The grandfather kissed his youngest grandson playfully, then they all gathered around the table in the middle of the sitting room, in front of the cake on which a photo of the smiling couple was printed.

"You won't start without me, right?"

Khatir descended from the upper floor while adjusting his white headdress, but all his efforts to fix his outfit for the special occasion were in vain. He kissed his father on the head, and his mother on the hand.

He had changed a lot since the incident with the water tank. He gained much more balance and common sense when his father got rid of the tank, and he became more attached to his father, who started to take him to social occasions. This had helped put him on the threshold of manhood.

They all sat to eat the cake, which they all took part in cutting. Jalal lifted his headdress over his head.

"Sara! Are there any plans for more grandchildren?," he asked.

Lameya looked at him reproachfully, while placing a piece of cake in Basim's mouth. Ali laughed and Lameya joined in with the teasing.

"The more grandsons you have, Jalal, the older you will look."

"When we talk about age, we refer to normal people who age with time and not those whose age has an inverse relationship with time," Jalal retorted, winking at his son-in-law, who turned to his wife to launch their usual round of family jokes about ageing. But before the sparring could begin, the doorbell rang. Khatir went to see who was there and returned quickly holding a white box.

"It was delivered by the postman," he said.

He placed the box on the table in front of Jalal. Surprised at what it could hold, he took the knife they used for cutting the cake and cut at the box until it opened. He looked inside and saw nothing but a small broken branch of a date palm tree. It was dry and withered, and beside it, there was a piece of paper. He unfolded it.

In the course of our life, we encounter two types of people. The first type are the ordinary human beings and the second type are those who are lame, like this old dried up branch of a date palm tree that died rather than give up its fruit. If it so happens that you come across one of these types, hold him tight. If he was doomed to choose between letting go of you and giving up his rights, losing his good name, or even dying, he would choose death rather than letting you down.

Shouldn't we celebrate every lame, then? Shouldn't we embrace the old lame as well?

Happy anniversary from your old friend, Ghassan Al-Kaheil.

Jalal inhaled a deep breath and his face beamed with a big smile. He held the old lame in his hands and contemplated it. He thought of Ghassan, who decided to go back to his work and travel despite all Jalal's attempts to convince him to stay. The two friends had hugged each other tight at the departure hall at the airport. He promised to come back soon. That farewell was two years ago, and he is still waiting for him to return.

Life in the house had settled after the storms that almost swept it away. During the immediate aftermath, Jalal worried about his old neighbour, Khalifa, who vanished suddenly. In the first few days after the incident, Khalifa would lower his head every time he saw him and quickly take a different path. He avoided him after prayers at the mosque. Then Jalal discovered that Khalifa had mysteriously moved away from the neighbourhood.

Jalal looked at his family who were gathered around him, laughing merrily. He looked at Lameya and her shining smile, then he sat back on the sofa and started humming his favourite song. A moment later, his son joined him in singing.

"I'm coming back to see you
I was driven by my longing
I'm wondering how you are
And how night influenced you…"

The end

Commentary

The real-life novel is the literary genre that gives the reader the best opportunity to live twice, in that they experience being another person, as the American literary critic, Gary Saul Morson, states. In order for the writer to present this rich experience to his readers, his work needs to have a great deal of credibility and reality.

From the perspective of moral responsibility and credibility, when recording historical incidents and documenting that particular era, I did my best to present true and accurate information found by digging deep into the available resources, such as TV interviews and official reports about the Mecca siege. Therefore, all the information mentioned in this regard, including the dates, details and names in chapter 15 of this novel, are all true and real without any alteration, interpretation, or amendment.

Finally, dear reader, it is hard to promise or claim that I have mentioned the whole truth, but I made sure that all of what I mentioned is true and accurate.

The author

Note of Thanks

I had the honour of meeting him for only one night. It was supposed to be a brief meeting, but our chat extended till the middle of that motivating night and granted me the privilege of knowing a new teacher, an inspirational mentor, a friendly advisor and a never-ending spring of creativity.

I extend my deep thanks, gratitude, and appreciation to the novelist Osama Al-Moslem for reviewing this book, giving invaluable feedback, and for writing about it. I was so blessed and privileged and honoured. My thanks to you.